Dem

By Christoph Paul

Printed in the United States of America

First Printing, 2014

The Only Rx Press

www.ChristophPaulAuthor.com

Table of Contents

"An artist is a creature driven by demons. He doesn't know why they choose him and is usually too busy to wonder why." **William Faulkner**

"Now, we've never actually tried to awaken a troll before from a Finnish Necronomicon, so please bear with us." **Nathan Explosion**

Demons In The TV

I'm demon hunting.

My momma said—well, she ain' t my real momma but she is the one I got now—she said we got demons in the TV. Well, I'm gonna catch these demons and send them back to hell, so I can watch some cartoons.

Ever since I left the orphanage and Miss Jones got me Baptized, I haven't watched one cartoon.

I liked the Baptism though, it felt good to get the water in my hair, swim in the lake, and let Jesus into my heart but I still really miss my cartoons.

I'd never tell Miss Jones this but I like watching cartoons more than hearing her read the Bible. Jesus is super nice and stuff but so is Captain Planet, but she says he's a homosexual communist.

We live out in Sanford, in Northern Florida, and tonight we got us one heck of a storm, which is why it's the perfect night for demon hunting.

They come out during the storms.

The TV don't work like usual cause Miss Jones got no cable, we don't even get that PBS show with them talking Muppets. The only thing we watch is just them old VHS tapes about Jesus and a little boy doing exorcisms but I noticed something weird before she put them tapes in; the TV changes when a storm comes and you can see the demons. They full of all these weird looking colors and make all these creepy noises.

They really are in the TV and I want them out. So, I got myself a plan to use the Power of Jesus to get them demons out of the TV.

I'm searching the channels right now to find them, but there's just a bunch of static.

I keep changing them and end up on one that's not all *staticky* and I see myself in the TV reflection. I look scared so I hold the bible up and nod to myself that I'm serving Jesus.

My cross swings back an' forth and it makes me feel good cause I look like the little boy in them exorcism tapes. I wish I could be like that little boy. I bet he watches all the cartoons he wants cause he got no demons running around doing demon stuff.

I know his TV is demon free cause I've seen him scare the heck out some demons in them VHS tapes.

I want a demon free TV too, so keep on searching and flip channels until I see something moving in the static; it's got weird colors and making weird noses too, sounds like the noises a demon would make.

It's definitely a demon.

My lord, protect me Jesus, it is a she; she is a devil—a she devil...oh my lord she is saying the F-word! She is moaning and screaming and saying the F-Word!

Only a demon says them kind of words.

She's one evil demon. She yelling too and making demon calls.

I can't be scared though; I must outsmart the She-Devil for Jesus and for Captain Planet. I remember the little boy tricking the demon, befriending it, and gaining its trust.

I can do it too.

I can be like the little boy.

I can be strong like him

I stay silent as the she-devil says, "Yes! Just like that, play with my pussy."

Oh Lord, Miss Jones told me about Demons being involved with goats, but not cats. Well, I love cats. I used to feed a pretty white one at my orphanage.

This demon must go, not just for Captain Planet but for the innocence of cats. I must exorcise this evil she-devil out of our TV.

I hold my Bible close and say to the Demon, "Hello, she-devil. I am here to save you and or send you back to Satan…"

"Yeah, you motherfucker; you like that pussy, don't you? Do it! Do it hard you motherfucker!"

"Demon, I forbid to you to curse. It is ungodly! And I do love cats. Soon that cat will be free. Cats are one of God's best creatures. And I will 'do it' demon. And to do it Demon, I'm gonna read a few words…."

"No, toss my salad, then I'll let you go all the way. I'll let you do whatever you want. Just toss the salad, now!"

"Salad...I didn't know you demons liked vegetables...."

"Ooh yeah, toss my salad, baby; good, do it. I need it."

"Fine, Demon, you can have your last meal before I use the power of Christ to exorcise you. I shall grab some from the kitchen."

I leave but hear her demon moans and satanic cursing follows me into the kitchen.

I gotta be super fast.

The she-devil keeps screaming as I open the fridge. Next to the milk is a big ole' head of lettuce. I grab it and run back to the she-demon in the TV.

I see her in the static, with more thunder coming she gets more clear: she all evil looking, with a pink and red color like a fire that only a demon could live in. There's another demon behind her; it could be a demon dog as it is sniffing her butt as the she-devil says, "Yeah you dirty ass-licker, toss my salad."

It is crude and my poor Christian ears hurt from hearing her dirty mouth, but the she-devil must not leave.

I must read the Bible and cast her on out of the TV.

"Um, yes, she-devil. I brought the salad. I shall toss it as you command and then you will know the power of Christ."

I take off the lettuces peels and toss them at the TV, "Here she-demon, here is your salad tossed."

I keep throwing it at the TV until the she demon says, "Ooh yeah, that is good. Yeah! Now lick it..."

"Lick it? Well, alright, she-demon, if that is what you need before being cast out, then I shall lick it and toss. And then you shall hear the word of the Lord."

I peel off the lettuce and start licking it as the she-devil screams, "Lick it. And toss it! Oh yeah, lick it, it's dirty!"

I do what demon tells me and lick the salad lettuce, she is right it tastes dirty and gross—figures a demon would like it; I then throw them lettuce pieces at the TV.

A few of them stick on screen and I tell her, "Alright demon, you have been fed, I have tossed the salad. Now I must read you something to *undemonify* this TV."

"Yeah! I want it hard. Put it in me. Go deep!"

"Yes, demon. I shall put the Lord deeply in side you."

"Yeah, give that dick good."

"Our Lord and savior is not that bad word she-demon. He is without sin. He is kind and loves us.

"Oh yeah! Make me cum! Go deeper, ooh fill me up; hit it right."

"Yes, she-devil, he will come and go deep! He'll fix your soul and make it right. He'll stop you demon....ugh, hold on, she-devil, I have to find the passage in the Bible and then you shall see His power."

I can't remember where in *Mark* it's about casting out them demons but I sure as heck know I'm on the right track. I keep on flipping through the chapter as the demon is screaming in pain—she can feel The Lord coming.

She keeps on screaming and I find the passage in Mark 16:17 and say, "These signs shall follow them that believe; in my name shall they cast out devils."

"Aw! Cum on my tits! I'm ready."

"Yes she-devil, Jesus will enter into your heart, under your breasts...He shall come. Through His name, I cast you out demon. In the Name of Jesus Christ I cast you out."

"Oh! My! God!" I hear behind me realizing it did not come from the demon.

I look behind me and see my step momma, Miss Jones holding her heart.

She's in shock as the she-devil says, "Oh, cover me with cum! Oh it's so good! Oh yeah, that big dick is a rocket full of cum. Put it all over my face."

"Oh Lord Jesus! Oh Lord." Miss Jones says and puts her wrinkled hands on her mouth looking all shocked.

I comfort her and say, "It is okay, Miss Jones, I mean, momma. I'm putting the demon under my control through the Lord's power. Praise his name. I'm exorcising the demon out of the TV, just like the little boy we watch. I'll be able to watch cartoons now."

"Ugh...boy...ma...ii...eart...hellll..."

Miss Jones ends up on the floor holding her chest; she starts shaking like a fish. Oh no, oh Lord Jesus, the demon is putting a spell on her; she is *Bibleless* and can't protect her soul. She said *hell* at the end; the she-devil is gonna try to take her there.

She shakes harder, like the people we see in the little boy's exorcism VHS videos.

The demon in the TV screams, "I'm cumming...oh yes, I'm so close, I'm almost there!"

Oh no, Lord Jesus, help us. Miss Jones is being taking over by the she-devil. She gonna take her to Hell, help me save her dear Lord.

I go to Miss Jones as she shakes; she puts her hand on her heart. She reaches at me with her other one and says, "Caaa....Caa..alll...ni...un...ugh"

Oh my Lord, she makes no sense. She is speaking in demon tongues.

I must save her.

I put the Bible against her forehead and act like the little exorcist kid on the tapes, "Demon, be gone. Leave my step-mother and go back to hell."

"Yes!" The demon screams with pleasure.

"Ugh....naw...ah..." Miss Jones gargles.

"I'll save you, Miss Jones. I'll save you with Jesus's help."

I put my cross against her head, "Through the power of Jesus, go back to hell, she-devil. You don't belong here, go back to the King of Lies."

Miss Jones' eyes peel back and gross demon liquid comes out of her mouth until she can't talk and stops moving.

The demon liquid still shoots out of her mouth and nose until she goes all still and I see the demon is gone. The she-devil is back in the TV moaning and talking about licking cats again.

I hold Miss Jones' hand and say a prayer to protect both of us. I ask the Lord to protect her and my soul.

When I finish the prayer; I notice her hand is still.

I feel her wrists like they taught me in orphanage. They ain't working right. The demon leaving her body killed her.

I kiss her forehead and shed a tear.

I never really liked Miss Jones, but she was a good lady and brought me to Jesus.

I love her, though. She was the only adult who was ever good to me.

It makes me sad that she's gone but happy cause I know I helped her get to heaven so she could be with Jesus.

The Led Zeppelin Shark Speaks

Author's Note.

Here is the mud shark's side of the story of the Shark Episode of Led Zeppelin. If not familiar please Google the story....

As you can see from *Googling* there was a sexual incident between Led Zeppelin, a shark, and a red head. While Led Zeppelin and the redhead groupie have different accounts we can now hear the truth from the animals side.

Here is the shark's tale.

****

How's it hanging dudes and duderinas; I am the most famous shark in the world. Seriously bro, I'm like only second to Jaws and that dude isn't even real; it's a total wash out holmes, the great whites get all the fish and the fame.

Me, I am just a regular mud shark, nothing special; I hunt minnows and eat baby snappers. The only real gnarly thing that ever happened to me (before I met Led Zeppelin) was I banged this white tip named Sheila. She was totally hot and cool and liked to hang out by Edgewater Hotel but she flaked out and skipped town to Cali.

Total bummer.

I waited around Edgewater for her to come back but my bro Jeffery swam by me and said he saw her on his vacay to LA going raw dog with some Hammerhead. My shark heart was broke.

I stopped eating and listened to that Beach Boys song "God Only Knows" just drifting like a dorkarino by the Hotel. It went on for a while bros and I call I could think of was Sheila; man, she was the best: her fin was the perfect size and she was a snaggletooth, which is just my thing—you know.

I wanted to die and prayed to Poseidon to take me out baby seal style.

But after a while bros, I just got the munchies hardcore and saw this squid floating in the water.

I shot right up and ate that spaghetti hot dog whole. It tasted good as balls man but when I went to swallow—total fucking wipeout, metal went through my gills and I kid you not bro all of a sudden I was flying in the air like those pelicans that chill by the pier.

Man, I just kept flying up and up; then these humans pulled me through the window in the hotel.

Crazy bro!

Even though I was super pissed I gotta say bros they were pretty gnarly looking humans: they had long hair that looked like a bunch of sea enemies and when I heard them talk they didn't sound like Seattle humans they had some weird Jacques Cousteau accent but way less lame.

But these rocker dudes weren't alone; on the bed was this redhead chick all nude-beach-like laying there spread eagle. Man, all I could do was flap around hoping to scare them but like a bunch of dicks they just laughed and asked her she was ready to have me take her to the stairway to heaven.

I prayed to Poseidon to make sure Sheila had a good life and made peace with you know deep stuff. I thought they were gonna make me shark sushi but these buttheads turned me into a dildo instead of a sea dish.

The one named Jimmy sang out, "here is a whole lot of love" as they had my shark fin rub on her tuna surprise. Even though I was scared as balls the smell of her just made me get the munchies. And this crazy chica was all into it like a clown fish and a sea enemy.

As they are having me black dog her taco I am seeing my life flash before my eyes: being a baby shark, eating baby seals, the time I wiped out on coral reef, and banging Sheila while the ginger colored human moaned all banshee style.

The louder she got the more I needed water; I made my final peace with Poseidon and closed my eyes for permanent wipe out.

But then I felt a big gush on my fins and into my gills.

I could breathe.

I opened my eyes and saw water shooting out of her clamshell. My fins got slippery this Jimmy dude laughed so hard that I flew out of his hands into air like Jonathan the lesbian seagull. I was flying bros but I thought it was my shark soul going to heaven but then I went down and hit the water and could breathe.

I was alive but I was not the same; I freaked out and swam down to Portland to get my head right.

I didn't talk to any other sharks for the next months; I just ate baby seals and tried to get my shit together. I'd get *sharkmares*, waking up wondering who these dudes were and why would they want a shark fin up in some human poon.

More months went by and I got bored and felt bummed. Even though I was scared and had the heebie-jeebies to go back to the hotel, I ran to this mud shark Brad and who told me he heard from the grapevine that my bro Jeffery had a nice stash of seaweed with shrimp.

That was all I needed to hear and left him in mid-sentence and swam back to my home and homies.

It took a good day and made my way toward the hotel and saw Sheila drifting.

She smiled at me and said, "Dude. I'm sorry. I got scared. I know Jeffery saw me with the Hammerhead and told you."

"It sucked dudearina; I really love you and stuff."

"I wasn't ready dude. I know it was bogus what I did, but still man, I always knew you were a special shark. When I heard what happened; I knew I was right."

"Heard what?" I asked, I didn't tell a soul about the hotel.

"Dude, about you hanging with Led Zeppelin; you are like the most famous shark in the world."

"Those dudes made me fin that chick?"

"Yeah, man they are the most famous humans in the world and they rock sonar style. Jeffery found a picture of you and the band and the ginger chick; he found it on the bottom of the floor. They must have taken it that night. Word has spread dude. Everyone wants to talk to you."

"Whoa, that is pretty gnarly."

"Yeah, man. Even the great whites want to talk to you..."

"I think those dudes are stuck up, but alright, I'd be open if they shared some yellow fin with me..."

Sheila then swam close to me and said, "I'm sorry dude. It really was bogus what I did. I don't want to mess with any more hammerheads; I am ready to have baby sharks with you. Can I get your love back?"

"Dudearina, you can have all my love."

The Masturbating Vampire

Val Cortez knew God's purpose for him was to save the souls of the savages, because he was once a savage.

He loved young female flesh and slept with many girls in northern Spain until one was with child. Not ready to be a father, he traveled by donkey down to the southern coast of Spain to escape marriage.

Southern Spain became a lonely place for Cortez.

He drank wine from morning to night to forget his failure to answer the call of fatherhood. He ended up destitute and near death when a nun found him on the side of the street.

She was not an attractive woman but he saw a new type of beauty that came from her offering food and salvation.

He bonded with the nun and enjoyed the teachings of the Bible. These teachings gave his life meaning and he felt special knowing God loved and forgave him. He made peace with his new life and developed a friendship of the soul with her.

The nun was proud of her pupil when he asked her if he should join the Church. She smiled and blessed his decision to go into the Priesthood.

The Church accepted Cortez but all the priest positions were taken in Southern Spain; the Church decided it would be best if he became priest of the first ship traveling to the New world. His assignment guided by the Holy Spirit was to travel to the Americas for gold and to save the savage souls.

Cortez accepted the position from the Church and was ordained. He felt blessed and ready to leave the past behind.

When he boarded the ship with the crew, he felt optimistic and enjoyed the smell of the sea. Inside the ship, one of his duties was to lead dinner prayer and after desert console the lonely seamen. His prayers, guidance, and empathy for the men helped the ship keep up morale.

The other men discussed missing their families and Cortez couldn't help thinking of his own child. He wondered what sex the baby was. Even being filled with the Holy Spirit he could not suspend the guilt he felt for abandoning the child.

Each night before bed, he prayed to feel less guilt. He asked God to take this guilt and transform it into more faith. It took time but as the ship approached the America's, Father Cortez was able to accept it was not in God's plan for him to be a father. The ship's men were his children and his job was to feed their souls and soon the savages.

When the ship landed, Cortez and his shipmates walked on to the New World's shore. It was as hot as Southern Spain but it had a different smell, unclean and wild like the brothels Cortez visited before the Holy Spirit saved him.

The people of the land were darker skinned with long hair and looked suspicious of the ship. Father Cortez said a prayer asking God to bless their mission. The other men walked off the ship holding guns and ready to conquer the coast.

Cortez's prayer was interrupted when the savages shot arrows at the lighter skinned intruders. The savage's arrows were not powerful enough to stop the magic black sticks of the Spaniards. Soon the coastal tribe was on their knees the way Cortez had his men kneel during Sunday service.

The Ship's soldiers took over the tribe grabbing their gold and bringing it back to the ship.

Days passed and the red skinned men and women became to weak to fight back; it was disease not the guns that took their fight away, as their immune systems became as weak as their bows.

The disease, a Spanish form of Small Pox, infected 2/3 of the tribe. They lost their strength and their heathen gods did not cure them nor did their Shaman who was also succumbing to the Spanish Small Pox.

The Shaman's rituals, mantras, and concoctions did nothing to stop the sickness of himself and his tribe. The Shaman was getting closer to death but Cortez saw him as a way to convert all of the tribe to Christians before they passed.

Cortez pulled the Shaman aside to talk with him in private under a palm tree.

He treated the Shaman with respect like he was an

equal. He had his translator explain the truth of Heaven, Jesus Christ, and that if the Shaman converted to Christianity and helped his tribe do the same he would sit at the right hand of God and never feel pain again.

He then paused and gave the shaman a solemn face and explained if he did not accept Christ and convert, his tribe they would all feel Hell Fire for eternity.

The shaman was starting to feel the pain as the disease mutated; it was affecting his blood flow giving the spiritual chief a burning sensation throughout his body. The Shaman started to crave the idea of an afterlife with no pain, for he knew death was coming soon.

He accepted Cortez's God and was the first of the tribe to be baptized. Afterward he told his tribe to accept the 'Jesus' as their God or else they would feel an even worse pain after they died.

The Shaman died a day later but Father Cortez was able to convert many red skinned savages offering them joys of Jesus's Heaven that Father Cortez described as an afterlife full of Gold, cold breeze, and all the fish and buffalo you could eat.

A week later after a Sunday Service on the shore, Father Cortez and the other Spanish settlers returned to Spain as most of the red skinned tribe had perished.

The Spanish Small Pox had mutated into a parasitic blood disease. The savages started cutting themselves to let out the 'fire blood.' With no Shaman and only a Bible in Spanish, a twenty-something boy who was not dying from the disease took the Shaman's place.

He cut the arms of his people and started sucking out the blood of the sick to see if it would cure them; he believed his body could handle their fiery blood.

It did, the disease affected the blood sucking stand in-Shaman in a different way: he did not die from the disease like the rest but instead his immune system developed strange symptoms to deal with the disease like being sensitive to sunlight and a craving more human blood to give the body Vitamin D and keep its telomeres from ending.

The disease became a mutated parasite that required human blood for nourishment, a disease that made a human host unable to die.

The parasitic disease also wanted to spread itself sexually; if no new human blood was ingested it would give a signal to the brain to release semen or it would make the host feel like their blood was on fire to reproduce itself.

Once the young Indian was fully *turned*, he desired blood and to spread the disease through his seed. He masturbated at first to feel less of the burn but it got tiresome and the thirst for blood got stronger.

He would not rape his people, he did not want to release this demon inside them and give them curse the white man gave him. Instead, he masturbated behind a palm tree until the sun went down. The few of members his tribe that were left were granted their wish for death as he sucked out all their blood and cooled his fiery blood.

When there were no more bodies of blood to suck, he cried as he masturbated onto their dead bodies.

After he climaxed again, he made a vow that if the white man's ship ever came again he would get revenge. He would turn the white man's shaman, who spoke the lies of The Jesus, into the same demon as him. He understood that the demon could be passed only through someone sucking on his blood.

The vampire Indian would give the white shaman the curse of the disease: the constant need to take life or release it from yourself.

He waited and hungered for more human blood and for revenge. He chronically masturbated waiting for the next ship of Spaniards to reach the shore.

Father Cortez was back on the ship heading to the same shore of the Vampire Shaman.

Spain and The Church were proud of him and his ship's progress. The Church funded a second mission to start a colony on the same coast. With no Indians left they could claim the land for the Catholic Church who would continue to help as long as the gold made its way back to Rome.

Father Cortez enjoyed the ship now had families aboard looking for a new start just like he received from the Church.

He would see the smiles of the children, and enjoy their innocence but yet there was still a part of him that wondered about his own child.

He'd have to say the Serenity Prayer and take solace in being the spiritual farther of the ship.

Like his soul, his child was in God's hand, which was better than his own. He was not returning to Spain and accepted and embraced being the Church's servant and priest of the New World Colony.

When the ship reached the same shore, the captain called everyone to the dining hall. He told Father Cortez and the rest of the passengers to wait until daylight to step onto land and reminded them they were blessed by God to arrive safely. He asked Father Cortez to say the night's prayer before everyone returned to sleep.

Cortez obliged and said a Hail Mary but a scream came from the inside of the ship stopping the sacred prayer.

Father Cortez looked under the moonlight and saw a young Indian on board; the longhaired red skinned boy was attacking the innocent by sucking blood from their necks.

Father Cortez recognized the young man; he remembered a boy that did not get sick from the disease, but he was no longer a boy—he was some type of demon who craved the white man's blood.

The families screamed as the soldiers from the Spanish Army shot their rifles and threw their knives at the Indian but nothing killed him. He took the stabbing and the bullets but still stood up right as he sucked the blood of the innocent.

Father Cortez made the sign of the cross. He asked God's for his protection watching blood spill out of the red skinned demon's wounds but be healed when he sucked on the new necks of the Spaniards'.

In horror, Cortez saw the red-skinned demon suck the children's blood out of their little bodies after he finished with their parents.

Cortez left his flock and ran to the back of the ship. He hid in the ship's modest chapel and heard more screams of the dying. He prayed to the God who had saved him before and he hoped would do the same again.

The young Indian had killed everyone. He made his way to the back of the ship's chapel where Cortez continued to pray. The vampire approached him with hate and bloodlust in his eyes. Father Cortez held his cross out for protection and prayed louder.

The young vampire took the cross out of his hand and threw it against the wall.

He growled at Cortez and said in broken Spanish, "Your people killed mine. You Christians said I go to hell. But I not die. I cannot die. The demon you preached about; it enter me. Now, demon makes me ingest blood or release seed. That is curse. To take life or let seed out. But curse can spread, if I suck your blood and make you suck mine—you shall be demon too."

Father Cortez begged the vampire in Spanish, "Please demon, don't make me into..."

But he stopped mid sentence as the vampire bit his neck and then put his own bloody wrist into Father Cortez's mouth forcing his 'demon' blood into Cortez's human body which was being drained of his own human blood.

The disease spread quick forcing Father Cortez's to desire more blood; he started suck harder on the Indian's wrist.

The blood trade finished.

Father Cortez was full of new diseased blood and the Indian felt no need to masturbate.

The young red skinned boy wiped the blood off his mouth. "Now, you will know the loneliness red man feels. When it is late at night and you masturbate and cry, know you deserve it."

The Indian left Father Cortez to find new blood or masturbate.

Father Cortez felt his heart beat with the new blood; it burned and he felt the burn the most in his crotch area. He needed to suck blood or to masturbate and release this 'burn' inside himself.

Cortez left the ship and walked onto the shore.

His senses were new and alien; his sense of smell and hearing increased as he heard and smelled the water washing against the beach while his massive erection pointed toward the trees.

A cute but wild dog came up to Farther Cortez, but he did not want to take any lives of God's creatures. He hissed at the dog and shooed him away. The dog whimpered and ran.

Cortez could not handle the burning sensation, he needed to release it; he grabbed his erect penis and started masturbating for the first time since he took the Priesthood.

It did not take much time as he came and the burn inside him cooled.

He wiped the semen off his hand with the leaves of a palm tree. He felt hatred for the Indian that made him this way; he felt existential loneliness as he was now a demon and believed he was no longer in God's good grace.

He contemplated about ending his life but knew that was the most mortal of all sins; deep down he knew he lacked the courage to do the deed. Even worse, he did not know how to kill himself, all he knew was he really wanted blood or to let his seed out on to the ground or inside a woman.

He called for the Indian speaking Spanish but the Indian did not return leaving Father Cortez with a loneliness and a desire for blood and masturbation. No one came to him, as the animals were the only sounds he heard.

Val Cortez was now alone in the coastal swaps of Florida and wondered if he was being punished for his past sins.

His philosophizing would only last so long as the cravings would come. He ended up masturbating ten times in three hours but the burn would return, for an act that felt new he was already sick of it.

He went out into the swamps to hunt accepting he would kill an animal for its blood. He went deeper into the swamps and found an alligator. He grabbed the six-foot gator and bit into his head sucking the blood out but it did not cure the need.

He needed human blood. The disease fed off and needed the DNA strands of human blood cells for nourishment.

He took his teeth out of the alligator and masturbated until he climaxed on top of the gator's head. The gator was in a daze but Val Cortez felt an existential ache that unless he found human blood, he would spend all of eternity masturbating.

For Val Cortez, time moved fast and slow; it does that when you're chronically masturbating. The years passed and the Americas became inhabited by more men and women from all parts of Europe and Africa.

Cortez still kept part of his human soul and morality; he knew if he got too close to human beings he would attack them. Instead he lived deep in the swamps where the moist air felt good for masturbation.

He masturbated through out the centuries, staying put in the swamps. He only took human blood twice: a dying southern solider during the Civil War who decided to spend his last moments in the swamps. Cortez saw the man suffering and sucked his blood until he crossed over.

The other time was once during the depression of the 1930's; it was a little boy who was malnourished and on the verge of death. He ran into the swamps to find food but was attacked by a gator. Missing a limb and about to die, Val Cortez sucked the boy's blood and then buried him giving him a Christian ceremony. The boy's blood tasted delicious and it felt good to not need to masturbate, but the sin of killing a child hurt the remaining bits of his soul.

He vowed never to suck human blood again. He cried heavy tears and masturbated thoroughly through the night.

More Europeans and Africans came to the Americas and more years passed for Cortez. He lived a purgatory existence of sleeping in the shade during the day and masturbating in the night. He would say his prayers after he climaxed and then go back to masturbating when the burn in his blood returned.

He stayed in the swamps of Florida but each year the swamp would get smaller and less wild. Until 500 years had passed.

The swamp had become so small he could smell human bodies from only a few miles away.

Civilization was encroaching on the swamp. A pit stop had been built less than a mile from Father Cortez's swamp-home; it had a gas station and a Taco Bell. He smelled the burritos and tacos from Taco Bell, which brought back his human memories of his old country of Spain. An even more potent smell was the fast food establishment's patrons with their fresh blood eating the food of his homeland.

He tried to masturbate to calm the cravings of memory and bloodlust but it was too strong. He climaxed and then walked out of the swamps wearing the same ripped rags of his priest uniform that clung to skin. He trudged through the road masturbating to the flesh and smell of old Spain.

When he reached the highway he saw a whole new world: mechanical donkey rides and magical lights. It wasn't just Satan that took over him, Lucifer now ruled the world as he saw women dressed scandalously who rode in strange-wheeled machines.

He craved the blood pumping through their flesh; he was given dirty looks by drivers as he masturbated and walked to the pit stop. He wanted blood or to leave his seed inside these women but the human that lived inside of him did not want to let the demon inside him win.

The closer he got to the smell of the Spanish food the more of his humanity he remembered. He thought of when he was a boy and his mother would make fresh beans and serve them with delicious avocados.

It brought him sadness as he cried and masturbated until he reached Taco Bell.

He walked to the drive-through where he saw a young pale but beautiful girl of Spanish decent who spoke in his native tongue tell him, "Please, I can't give out any food...and you can not do that in public."

He looked at her and stopped masturbating. It was strange but he did not want to suck her blood; though, he still wanted to masturbate. He wondered if it was love at first sight that overpowered this urge to attack her.

He nodded his head and went and masturbated in the Taco Bell dumpster.

He kept on masturbating when he felt a trash bag hit his arm and stop him from climaxing; he looked up and saw the girl from the drive-through window.

She starred at him with his penis in his hands but was not startled and told him in Spanish, "It is okay. I know who you are; I know you have the burn in your blood. Come home with me. You will shower. You need it and then we shall talk."

Val Cortez was in shock and could only nod his head in agreement.

He loved being near someone and not craving the need to suck their blood. He loved too that she was so kind hearted. It had to be love; he wondered if she was angel walking the earth.

He stopped masturbating and she escorted him to her

car.

They arrived at her apartment that had oriental blinds all around the windows that she bought at Ikea. Val Cortez did not understand why a girl of Spanish decent would have Asian material but he also could not understand why he did not want to suck her blood.

She smiled at him and said, "It feels good, right."

"What does senorita?"

"To not want to suck the blood of someone you are standing next to."

"Si, how do you know? How do you know what I think and feel; are you a witch or an angel that can the read the mind?"

"No, I know because I am like you. I am a vampire, one who consumes blood or engages in lust to the stop the burn."

"Vampire?"

"That is what we call ourselves, there are more of us now, you must have been one of the first. Where have you been? It's like you know nothing of the modern world?"

"I do not know much senorita; I have lived in the swamps for many years. I have been…a vampire for hundreds of years; I have lost count how many years. I don't suck blood; not anymore. I masturbated many times, for many years. How long have you been a…vampire?"

"I have been one a long time too; I came to the New World, to find family but became a vampire instead."

"Was it an Indian that *turned* you?"

"No it was a ex-Catholic Spanish nun, from the old world. We did very bad things. Lesbian things. Afterward she sucked my blood as I sucked hers. I *turned*. She stayed with me and we masturbated together as we squirted to stop the blood lust. She then abandoned me and I have been fending for myself ever since. "

"I forgive you."

She laughed and said, "You forgive me?"

"I was a priest once, but now...now, I'm not; I still forget sometimes. But now, with you; I feel something. Something like love. I have felt unimaginable loneliness, the absence of God and man. I want and need a partner. Someone who understands. Someone to love and love back. Maybe we can masturbate together, or even make love; you can squirt and I can release seed to keep up us from sucking blood. We can try to be less sinful and still serve God even if we are demons."

"I don't want to suck blood anymore either. And I have been lonely too. The human that lays cold inside me feels something toward you. Something like...a connection."

She let out a tear; Father Cortez wiped it off and told her, "It is okay. We are both good Spaniards that have demon blood but we can make a Heaven of this Hell with one another. You are beautiful; already the short contact with you has made me fall in love. I love you. I could give up blood but I could not go another day without you near me and I don't even know your name."

"I've met a few others, vampire, but I never felt the human connection like I do with you. Let's not masturbate. Let's make love. Names do not matter, what we feel does."

"Si, mi amore."

"Si."

They took off all their clothes and he entered her. They felt a peace and pleasure that the disease had taken from them. Her vagina was tight, reminding him of the young girls he once made love to. He remembered why sex was better than masturbating and the disease inside him enjoyed the feel of a vagina instead of a hand.

They had passionate sex for five minutes until Val Cortez and the young but old Spanish girl both came and both felt satisfied.

He knew they would have to do it again but it was ok, he felt in his heart he would never tire of making love to this beautiful vampire and he could finally live in peace without God or his humanity.

Him and her could just be.

She put her head on the crook of his chest and smiled. He looked in her eyes and smiled back. There was something special about them; he would have felt connected to her even as a human.

He put his hand through her hair, "I will love you for

eternity."

"I will too, mi amor. I don't feel the need to masturbate or suck anyone's blood right now, the warmth of your love and semen inside me quenches my blood thirst."

"Si, me too, senorita."

"My life as a human was hard too; I was abandoned and have always felt alone. I've been searching for a love like this for a long time."

"I felt the same, that is why I joined the Church. Loneliness is the worst pain. Why did you feel so alone when you were human? Who abandoned you?"

"There was a loss I had felt for centuries. It was the loss of a family member. I finally feel some peace about it, now that I found you."

"Who was your family? We have the same dialect from Spain, maybe I knew them long ago" Val Cortez asked, though, he was more preoccupied with the future as he pictured a blissful eternity with the girl.

He thought of even starting a family, wondering if they could even have a demon child.

She smiled and with a tint of sadness she said, "My mother died when I was young. I was a bastard. My father was named Val Cortez; I heard he went to the new world but was never found. It is ok; I found you."

She smiled and kissed his breast where his heart beat the diseased blood through out his body. The peace he felt was gone as she held him closer.

He would not tell her, he couldn't. She looked too happy and he could not break her heart again. He was going to suffer for all of his sins for eternity.

He held back tears as she smiled and bit into Cortez's chest needing to feed the baby that was forming inside of her.

Christophous

I'm at my desk alone in my apartment. I look at my Amazon sales ranking on my laptop and see it has hit its plateau.

I am dropping each hour.

It frustrates me that books with shirtless fireman on the cover that are masturbatory fodder for housewives are doing way better than my own books.

It feels like God is punishing me for working at the porn store in DC. I did sell a lot of porn, so this could be a message from Him.

Is this a symbolic act of spiritual punishment? Being fucked over for selling fuck tapes?

God is probably not a fan of my writing either and I'm sure Jesus doesn't appreciate the title *The Passion of The Christoph.*

I am "of the Devil's Party" like Blake said, which sounds cool but being broke sucks.

I decide not to turn to God to console this crappy feeling and instead turn to His Adversary and say to my empty room, "Satan, help me out. I'm struggling. I'd honestly give you my soul for more book sales."

My room shakes and then my computer goes from Amazon rankings to YouTube. The Video for *Running with The Devil* by Van Halen begins to play.

It's scary but kind of cool and out of thin air, Jonathan Franzen appears and I say, "Franzen? What the hell?"

"My friend, call me Lucifer, and Hell, that is where I came from."

"Whoa, you're really Satan?! You exist!"

"The one and only, but don't tell anyone. I like ambiguity. I'm like the chicken store owner meth Drug Pin in *Breaking Bad*."

"Yeah, that character was bad ass. But why do you look like literary novelist Jonathan Franzen?"

"Because your sin of envy and pride has me take his form, Christoph. You wish to be a great literary superstar and your pride is acting out because shitty books are doing better than yours."

"They are really shitty, Satan, there's some serious crap in the literary world, it does hurt my pride."

"I know, they are definitely shitty, let me tell you a secret; God is a fan of writing hence Him writing this whole Bible thing. But all those hacks have a special place with me; their punishment will be to read their worse 1 star Amazon reviews for all eternity."

"Well, that is good to know, at least there is some justice. Thanks for coming when I called."

"I heard your call and now I am here to make a deal."

"You want my soul in exchange for literary fame?"

"Christoph, dear Christoph, don't be foolish. I already have your soul. All the terrible things you have done as a teenager; you are definitely of the Devil's Party. And did you think when you used Twitter to have sex with that lonely poet from Eastern Europe who was visiting NYC, there would be no repercussions? That sealed the deal. God won't forgive anyone for using social media to get sex. It will be an 11th Commandment in time."

"Yeah, that was pretty screwed up, I should have called her the night after but you know...she got clingy."

"Bitches be spooky, Christoph, I was there when Eve ate the apple."

"True, but still, why are you here Lucifer if you already going to get my soul?"

"Contrary to popular belief, I am a humanist and a big fan of the arts (though I despise post-modernism since I find it very trite). Who do you think inspired rock and roll, existentialism, Cable TV, and stuff that is just dope, yo?"

"I thought maybe God did."

"Come on, Christoph, you've read the Bible; He is a Republican philistine. He's a tight ass and Jesus, though a good poet is too self-involved. And just to set the record straight, I did not inspire Mohammed in *The Satanic Verses*. Rushdie was just starting shit to sell books."

"Word. But if you already have my soul why are you here? Oh, and could I hang with Marilyn Monroe, like when I'm in Hell and stuff?"

"I got you, dog, nicest ass in hell until Kardashian comes down. But back to earthly matters, Christoph, I am here because I am fan of you, Christoph; ironically, I am here to lead you not into temptation. That is the deal."

"Really? You're a fan? Thanks, Lucifer, that means a lot. I appreciate that...wait, what is my temptation?"

"Your stuff is cool Christoph, but I see you slipping and losing patience. I see you wanting to give up on your ideals and write lame books and sell out. Today, you even *DMed* links of your book on Goodreads, which is just not cool. *DMing* that your book is free today is the equivalent of unwanted anal sex, which is even a sin I even find repulsive. You are on your way to being a good writer Christoph, but you need to have some pride in your work, it is decent and deserves better treatment from you."

"I know...I'm just frustrated and I want to break through and make some money and I have this new idea that I think will sell 'Just Because He Likes Your Facebook Status, Doesn't Mean He Likes You.' I mean, have you seen the top free and non-free 100 Books on Amazon? Seriously lame books. I mean, come on Lucifer; do I have to write crap just to get people to want my book even when I'm giving it away for free? I know I'm a newbie and lack patience, but I just want to break through...this Facebook book could be the next 'He's Just Not That Into You.'"

"Shame on you, Christoph, for even thinking of writing such crap and I saw you even tweet that title."

"I know, I even thought about coming up with an outline."

Satan/Franzen wags his finger at me with disapproval and says, "No! You will stop this at once, Christoph. You will not put out another book playing on women's insecurities. I, Satan, even feel bad about the Eve shit."

"So what do I do Satan?"

"You keep writing what you are writing and be patient, Christoph, I have plans for you. Music was not your main path, but you lead me to Sean Quinn Hanley who will make rock n roll good again. But you, Christoph, you're here to write books that will make the literary world less lame."

"I know, Sean is bad ass, we are in agreement there but it's been hard finding that audience. I'm getting there little by little. Maybe I really should get an agent?"

"I don't even deal with literary agents they are even too evil for me, but you need them for foreign rights—I can even find me in those details. But for now, you must accept you have fans, myself, and others are finding your work. You see; I am selfish, for I am the Devil, but here's the thing: God is getting all the good writers. I found out that Phillip Roth is going to Heaven (there is a Jewish clause for those born before the 1950s, it's a long story.) I need more cool writers in Hell; it gets lonely and uninspiring. All I'm getting is romance and lame erotica writers—it's fucking lame bro."

"Damn, but that is cool for Roth, he's pretty good."

"He is but you are getting there Christoph. You are not Roth but if you keep at it you can be also be a self-important literary Jew too. You have chutzpah and the chops. It will just take time and winning one fan at a time."

"Thanks man, you know, you are right Satan, and I do have some fans and supporters already; it's cultish and small but people are digging what I am doing. It is different but they appreciate it even if it's just in small doses."

"Christoph, you, will be a little dirty needle that just needs to be spread everywhere so people will step on it and get addicted. You just need to keep writing for that to happen."

"Whoa, Lucifer, that was like a really poetic metaphor. That is pretty insightful."

"That is why the poet is of the Devil's Party."

I laugh and smile at Satan and say, "Thanks Satan, I appreciate it."

"Your welcome, Christoph."

"I feel a lot better. Lucifer, I really appreciate you taking the trip but if you don't mind would you please take off Van Halen. I got some writing to do."

"That's the spirit, Christoph. I'll see you in Hell."

Abortion on Aisle 12

Kill two fetuses with one shopping cart was what Billy thought as he walked through Whole Foods.

Not much of a healthy eater and by no means one to need to buy organic, Billy was there because he had a plan to get him and his pregnant junky girlfriend Rita some cash and a free abortion. He also noticed walking through aisle 9 that Whole Foods had 30% off on organic pumpkin seeds but the thought of eating made him want to puke.

Heroin withdrawal always reminded Billy of when he went deep-sea fishing with his drunk of a father.

He was feeling the shakes along with nausea.

He didn't like the smell of Whole Foods but they picked it over Trader Joe's because their parking lot had more 2014 Lexus and Prius Hybrids.

Billy and Rita had no cash and were fiending hard. Once Rita hit the third trimester with twins they knew something had to be done as she was shooting up for three.

Rita and Billy thought about selling the twins to Pro-Life people or infertile couples but neither would really pay much for junkie babies. With all the smack Billy and Rita did, they thought the twins would be born conjoined and/or retarded.

Thinking of the twin fetuses messed up made it easier for Billy to get rid of them but that wouldn't erase the fact that they still needed cash and they had gotten too used to buying quality heroin from their Afghani neighbor Talib.

Billy never had much business sense but he felt a little pride for coming up with this 'genius-ass' plan of getting a yuppie at Whole Foods to give his girlfriend an abortion by shopping cart and then have the yuppie give them guilt and liability money.

He didn't want much, just some money on the spot so he could pay Talib for an eighth and monthly payments to help him and his lady deal with their pain and suffering that would also go to Talib.

Billy felt this plan was solid and simple but walking through Whole Foods the last half-hour he was seeing the actual implementation of the plan was way harder than he thought.

His girlfriend was supposed to be by the cage-free eggs across from Aisle 12, but she didn't like the cold; it made her nipples hurt. She went over to the fruit area and started stealing individual blackberries.

Billy had thought Rita was becoming a shitty girlfriend; she used to give excellent head (which was how they paid for heroin sometimes, though Talib was strangely religious and didn't accept the offer) and had an eating disorder so she was low-maintenance, but her being pregnant with twins affected her fellatio skills (the nausea) and biology overpowered psychology and the twin fetuses demanded food to be eaten.

She was becoming baggage and the Whole Foods Abortion plan was the only thing that was going to keep them together, but instead of standing were she was supposed to she was stealing and eating blackberries. He knew she was not wife material because she would skimp bags. Before heroin, stealing was her drug of choice.

Billy felt annoyed at her like usual: it wasn't hard what she had to do; she just had to stand there and look innocent and *miscarriagey*. At least she was staying in one place, he now just had to find someone who looked like they had money and bump in them at the right time and angle.

If he did it right they'd let go of their cart and it would smash into Rita's stomach and all would be solved.

Who would be this person be to cause miscarriage by carriage?

Billy kept stalking people, looking for who would be startled the easiest; the problem with the Whole Foods shoppers was their love of organic meals and yoga practice gave them a great sense of calm.

He was feeling great concern he wouldn't find the right mark until he saw a woman who looked frazzled and full of fear. There was a paranoia to her that attracted Billy like a predator looking for easy prey. She was old too and resembled the mother from the Brady Brunch.

Wait a second! On a second glance Billy thought it was definitely the actress Florence Henderson who played Mrs. Brady. Billy knew her features intimately because he jerked off to a rerun once and he never forgot a face he masturbated to.

Billy was impressed that Mrs. Brady had aged quite nicely but then he remembered this was not about reliving his childhood it was about getting rid of children he didn't want and money for heroin.

Watching her arthritis-like movements Billy knew Mrs. Brady was the perfect person to cause his girlfriend a miscarriage; not only could they get money from her but tabloids would pay big time as well.

Billy for the first time in a long time felt something like gratitude toward God but then remembered God probably didn't approve of having Florence Henderson give your girlfriend a third-trimester abortion.

Instead he took this moment, as much needed luck and knew he had to follow through with the plan.

He looked in her cart; it was full of all the food groups except fruits and vegetables. He saw Mrs. Brady was heading there as she passed Aisle 12.

Billy hated math but this was a real life situation that involved using it by adding angles and speed and all that kind of stuff.

He knew he had to go right, walk fast, and be in area by the bananas and pineapples before Florence Henderson arrived.

He darted around Aisle 13, passed his junkie girlfriend still eating the blackberries, and made it to the bananas in 13.3 seconds.

He was in the right position; he had a few seconds before Miss Brady would arrive. To increase the odds of the plan, he pushed a couple bananas peels on the floor and kicked them to where Miss Brady's cart would be. He wasn't sure if it would really help but he had seen this act pulled off successfully in most of his favorite cartoons.

Mrs. Brady arrived right on time as Billy bumped right into Florence Henderson, not even needing the banana. These type of cart collisions caused an average of 15 injuries a year at Whole Foods.

It was a hard impact and Miss Brady's cart flew out of her hands taking angle that increased the amount of kinetic energy and speed landing right on Rita's stomach.

The six-month twins were dead on impact from the cart hit; an unexpected pain came to Rita and she fell to the floor.

Rita looked up and screamed for help toward her boyfriend; he stood in nausea watching his girlfriend spit up blood from her mouth while other blood fell from between her thighs.

Florence Henderson lunged to toward Rita to help but her leg got tangled with Billy's and she fell straight to the floor; Billy tripped over her foot and tried to keep his balance but stepped on one of the banana peels causing him fall face first into the upright pineapples.

His last thought was *I'm going to die by a pine...*but his thought stopped as his nose hit directly on the hard outside of the pineapple making it go straight into his brain.

Another pineapple spike went right into his eye.

His body went limp and rolled to the floor with the organic Hawaiian pineapples sticking out his face still attached to his eyeball.

His body stopped rolling and ended up next to Rita's feet as all the Whole Fooders screamed including Florence Henderson.

Rita was also soon to die; she was losing too much blood.

She looked up at the horrified faces and Mrs. Henderson gave her a look of pity. Rita never told Bill, but she loved the *Brady Bunch*. Before she started stealing, she watched reruns before school and always wished she had a family like that instead of a stepfather who liked to touch her at night.

With tears coming down, she held Mrs. Brady's hand, and said, "Remember the vase-breaking scene, when the kids hid it from you and the water came out during dinner from the broken vase? I'm like that vase. I'm broke, I always was; I wish you had been my mom, I wouldn't have ended up so broken."

Hustle and Fly

Bitches ain't shit but hoes and breadsticks. That is on the real motherfuckers; I've been pigeon pimping since a nigga's feathers turned red. Shit, while all these other herb birds are hanging in the park shitting on statues, I'm flying to the back alley behind Nino's pizzeria on St. Marks.

It's dem breadsticks' yo, my pigeon bitches is hooked on that shit; these hoes be strung out on these garlic rolls—foe show. I protect these pigeon-heads and make sure all niggaz be getting fed.

All these other pussy ass pigeons living on Front Street know not to come here and start shit. I'm mother fucking strapped with a 12 cm beak. My hoes know I'll peck a nigga's eyes out whose fronting.

First they pay and then they get that pigeon-pus-say! And business is booming and blowing up; this pimp game is filling up a nigga's belly and shit, with all these park pigeons with no game and light feathers, they all bringing us Korzo Burger left overs to get feather deep in my pretty peeps—I'm *ballin*; the more food they bring the more my hoes will ruffle their feathers yo. These hoes go crazy for them Dream Balls that cracker ass chef Steven makes.

Motherfucker is an artist; straight up Nino Brown of hamburgers.

But yo, on the real, it wasn't always like this; back in the day when I was a lil' baby bird nigga there was no need for pimping, slanging, and hoeing. We'd all just chill at Tompkins Square Park and that cracker ass Steven would just throw out his left overs and we could all get our fair share; *pimpadelic* pigeons like me would just get all that pussy cause I got that big beak. Shit was dope. To drop some knowledge—it was Darwinian, yo.

But that shit all changed when Marquis De Hawk moved up to Tompkins square Park...shit was never the same when we saw that Debo sized nigga fly in and perch up them Tompkins Square trees. For real, yo, a hawk; a straight up gangsta hawk. On his first day that nigga ate 3 pigeons and a squirrel. It was like Omar from *The Wire*, yo—no pigeon felt safe. We had to start running in packs and the food supply went down.

This crusty greyback named Jamal moved in on Korzo and set up shop with some pretty feather bitches and me, I did Nino's. I got a bunch a little baby bird soldiers to match Jamal's to spread the word that I got those bright feather bitches. Still, I gotta watch these little pawn nigga pigeons cause I know they want my crown.

Shit, on the real, why I'm telling you all this is cause I want out of the game. For real. The pussy, the Dream Balls, and even the power—it's got no end. I've seen *The Wire*; there ain't no niggaz like Marlo, in the end we all just Stringer Bells.

I'm gonna get pecked to death by my hoes or by that busta ass nigga Jamal; I put a hit on him but the bird hit the wall and Jamal tortured and then killed him.

I know he is waiting to beak me to death.

I was sure that was my fate but then I met this fly ass piece of pigeon pussy. This pigeon was banging, yo. I thought she was slumming for some pizza; I'm talking quality upper west side type of bitch. On the real, I caught the vapors and started chirping (I never chirped once for a bitch, never had to cause I got that big beak) singing pretty Rihanna type shit.

She came over and I was ready to tap it but she gave me a dirty look and told me, "I am not that type of pigeon and I am spoken for. My boyfriend Carlton and I are in court phase."

"Then why you up in a nigga's face if you ain't gonna let me ruffle them feathers, yo."

"You are disgusting and rude; I also have a name. It is Dominique. I shouldn't even tell you why I am here, but your 'friend' Ronnie quit our singing group on the upper west side and recommended you as a replacement. I promised him I would check you out. We are having tryouts in a month, to renew our lease...You will need back up singers. Maybe your 'lady bird friends' can help you."

Some herb bird flew up with a big ole' dream ball in his mouth, dropped it, and said, "Damn yo, she extra fine. I'll give you the whole ball if I can hit that shit."

The fine ass Upper West Side honey rolled her eyes. "Gross. Think about it Pasquale. You have something special, Ronnie was at least right about that."

She flew away and I pecked this herb bird in his grill and said, "Get the fuck out of here nigga!"

He flew too and I was left with my bitches, his Dream Ball, and my thoughts.

Ronnie was my boy, we go back and shit; he let a lil' nigga crash by his tree after my moms died. That fool said I chirped in my sleep and it was all-pretty and shit; I thought that nigga was playing, but he was keeping it real—damn, he did say his word was bond.

As my top 3 hoes started eating the Dream Ball and I looked out from the alley and that Debo motherfucker Marquis De Hawk was looking my way.

I knew this was it; this was my chance to get out of the ghetto.

I had to take it. That's on the real.

I turned back to my hoes and said, "Bitches, stop eating. All 3 of you...Alright hoes, you ain't gonna be tricking no more."

The bitches looked shocked but they listened so I didn't have to raise my pimp wing and continued, "I want out of this game; I want the good life. I want that Upper West Side life. I can chirp. I didn't even know it; but I can spit this poetic pretty shit. You gonna be my back up bitches. We gonna do this shit."

Chantal my number one hoe gave me the last bite. I chewed down and finished the Dream Ball; then told her and the other two hoes, "Practice starts now. We got new Dream Balls to chew down on. The ones that will take us out of the ghetto."

This chirping shit was hard at first and my pimp wing was used many times but after a few weeks I turned these hoes into respectable chirpers.

When the day came for the tryouts; I saw Marquis De Hawk eating some little Squirrel and we flew the coup.

It took a good hour but we made our way to the Upper West Side. It was by some little cafe where they had these bomb ass bread sticks, the shit smelled clean—that Organic shit, yo, you only find on the upper west side.

I saw Dominique perched next to some herb bird and I chirped and then my bitches followed. I could see the humans impressed as they threw dope ass food at us to eat. Dominique looked happy but that herb bird next to her was all smug and shit, "He is good enough to be my understudy Dominique, I am still the lead."

"I agree. I am very proud of you, Carlton. Your have progressed with your Jealousy issues."

This smug ass nigga Carlton smirked at me and said, "I am not concerned about this little hood rat."

"Nigga, please. We all know you know I'm a starter and you second string. You gonna be replaced by me."

Carlton rolled his beady pigeon eyes and says, "I don't know if he is right for the group. I think we can find a more appropriate understudy."

Dominique looked at me and I begged her with my eyes to give me a chance, "Carlton, let's let them stay here for tonight. He can try again tomorrow and then we can do our duet."

"Fine." Carlton said while starring at my hoes.

We camped out on the upper west side but I knew I had to handle this Carlton shit; I knew that Dominique was making him wait to hit it and his little blue balls were probably about to burst yo.

I told my hoes what to do—they pros, foe so.

I went and found Dominique practicing solo and said I needed a private word with her. She said ok and I took her aside, "Look, I know you think I'm just some hood nigga, but I appreciate what you are doing for me and shit. But on the real, I gotta tell you; I don't trust Carlton. I think he ain't what he seems."

"Pasquale, stop assassinating Carlton's character. He's a great pigeon. I think you are jealous."

"Maybe, yo, but I saw him looking at my hoes. The way many man pigeons do—I'm just saying yo, be careful."

I saw her look worried; she looked so fine with her feathers all ruffled and said, "Okay, fine. Let's go check on Carlton and see he is resting up for tomorrow."

We flew over and saw that nigga was having a threesome with my top 2 hoes. My number one was tossing his little bird salad, while he was tearing the other one up *pigeonstyle*—it felt too good for him stop.

Dominique shed a little bird tear and screamed, "All of you out! All of you. I will perform with Pasquale. Carlton, you have broken my heart."

He looked upset but my hoes fuck so good he couldn't stop and I said, "When you bitches are done, take him back to the ghetto; y'all work for Carlton now. I'm quitting the game for good."

Dominique flew away and I followed her fine ass all the way to Central Park. Never seen it before it; it was *ballin*. She landed in some big ass tree and I saw her sad eyes in the moonlight—the bitch looked beautiful. In that moment, I knew I was gonna marry her ass and then fuck her Akon-style in this park—word is bond.

"What's up girl. You sad and shit?"

"Yes Pasquale. Of course I am."

"Fuck that nigga."

"I never did. I was waiting to be married. I want marriage and Carlton I guess didn't."

"Look, yo, I never chirped for nobody until I saw you Dominique. I thought love was some pussy ass nigga bullshit but that thinking that was the bullshit..."I then got down on one leg, "Dominique, after we win the competition tomorrow and we are *ballin*, will you let me do you proper and marry me up in this park. You the one, girl. For real."

"Are you ready to change, Pasquale and be a good man to me?"

"Word is bond, yeah, I'm ready. I got love for you. On our wedding day, I am going to tell you something my ma asked me before she died. I couldn't answer the question but now I can yo, because of you."

She let out another little tear, smiled, and said, "I feel it too about you; I felt it when you first chirped. I will mate with you and be your wife."

"Word, girl."

We slept in the tree, feather to feather; it was the bomb—shit felt so good yo. We woke up in the morning, practiced our routine, and then went to the cafe ready to win that motherfucker.

All the other pigeons were there and we knew if we sang the best, we could have bomb ass breadsticks for life. I looked at my fiancé, she looked finer than a mother fucker, so I started chirping; we did a duet of Marvin Gaye's and Tammi Terrell's 'You Are All I Need to Get By' and we fucking killed it.

We made it rain breadsticks.

We won. We owned it. We now had a spot to eat and we had a home—that tree we slept in. I made it out of the ghetto and was ready to be a good man to Dominique. Life was dope, can't even front, a nigga felt happy for the first time ever in his life.

We had our wedding day at the park; my hoes even showed up with Carlton, that herb bird almost looked as happy as me; I could see the pimp game suited him. Dominique looked super-fine, she even had her little sister Tamika there; she was a good girl. I felt ready to be family man and take care of my ladies... not hoes; out of love and respect for Dominique I stopped saying bitch, nigga, and hoes. Love can change man—word is bond.

We said our vows and I went to grab the ringworm from Tamika to give to Dominique when I looked up and saw that crusty grey back Jamal flying at me and Tamika.

That fool calculated wrong and was gonna hit Tamika. I saw the fear of Dominique of losing her sister and I jumped in front and took a beak right in the chest—a damn beak-by, on my wedding day.

As Jamal flew away while screaming, "Now we even nigga, you stupid if you think you can't escape the ghetto shit you did."

Then he was gone; I saw Tamika was alright but I felt the pain—he got me good.

Dominique came to me and I could see in her eyes she knew I was going to die. I hated seeing her like this and I told my beautiful wife, "It'll be a'ight. You'll be fine. I'm gonna be ok."

She cried and rubbed her feathers against mine and said, "Just breathe baby, it'll be ok. He didn't get you that..."

She couldn't finish the line, she knew it was lie; we didn't have much time as she said, "Pasquale, I love you...please tell me...what was the question, you can now answer that your mom asked you."

I could feel my heart slowing down and a tear falling out for the first time ever in my life and told her, "My moms asked me if whether if I wanted to live or die...I now know I want to live, but my love, it's now too late..."

The Haunting of The Paranormal Romance Awards

It was the moment they all had all been waiting for at RomCom: who would win The Haunted Heart Award for Best Paranormal Romance Novel. The competition was stiff involving *Angels in Chains* by Cynthia Eden, *Immortally Yours* by Angie Fox, *Mark of the Witch* by Maggie Shayne, and *My Husband Never Left* by newcomer Shira Constantine.

My Husband Never Left was different than the other novels. While they had their typical plots of vampires, spirits, and angels who fell for a fictional female protagonists, Shira said her book wasn't a novel at all but a memoir—though her editor, publisher, and psychiatrist felt it would be better if they presented it as fiction.

But it was real to Shira.

She wrote with passion and honesty about how her dead husband loved her so much he haunted her home and ravished her at night while other lonely ghosts and spirits watched.

It was a touching if not slightly kinky love story that many housewives and teenage girls enjoyed. While her book used the same amount of melodrama and lackluster style of writing, her book stuck out—it felt real.

It also had more literary quality: the ending was not the typical 'they lived happily ever after', instead it left a question on how her husband and his lost spirit friends could enter the living world as one being.

Many assumed it would be a series.

The rest of the paranormal romance writers found the book and Shira very strange (along with her outfit as she looked like a gothic lunch lady), yet the story was special and it was making more waves on twitter and paranormal romance chatrooms than all the other books combined. There was an animosity toward Shira from the other writers because in their own haunted hearts that knew Shira wrote the best book— even if it was really weird.

Shira believed this too and was told by her spirit husband that if she won, the spirit world would let him and the other ghosts become real. She wanted this more than anything. She sat and waited for this moment along with the other paranormal romance writers who sipped their martinis and wine glasses.

They kept on drinking when hunk and host Fabio returned to the stage and said into the microphone, "Aw, yea, everybody, we having such good time; so many nice prizes for so many nice books. Our next award I can relate to cause I'm old I am getting so close to death, ah-ha-ha-ha. But I still have such great hair. The award is for Best Paranormal Romance Novel of the year and our special guest and presenter is

Amanda Hocking. Aw, she so beautiful, give her a round of applause."

Amanda walked up wearing a casual white t-shirt that said *I Suck* with a flew drops of blood falling from the letters and a black pantsuit. Fabio gave her the stage and most of the women in the audience gave him their eyes. Even when they were little girls they snuck books with him on the covers finding a magical world, that most of their husbands could not provide when they became adults.

Amanda cleared her throat and the women looked at her with envy and awe, "Hello, it is so cool to be here. I was a winner before and I am excited to hand over the torch of being totally cool and loved by the spirit world."

The audience all laughed except the nominees, they were too nervous as the event was being live tweeted and the winner would get a big boost in their Amazon sales.

Amanda then read the names and there were the standard claps until she said Shira's name and her book title, the claps became half-hearted as Shira talked to her dead husband (which is still not appropriate to do even at the paranormal romance awards), "Our love and your restless soul will be consummated with this award. It will free you and our love will be tangible and we will feel peace."

The Romance writers heard her and thought she was being really inappropriate and just really weird; they marketed themselves as weird but that was because many of their publicists wanted to make sure they got the *Hot Topic*ers because they had more money to spend than even the house wives.

Shira started saying a bizarre Wiccan chant which made the room feel ever more uncomfortable. Amanda Hocking and the others tried to pretend she wasn't there as she finished saying the nominees.

Shira stopped the prayer when Amanda Hocking announced, "And our winner for best paranormal romance novel...oh, it was my favorite too. *Immortally Yours* by Angie Fox."

There were loud claps and cheers. A smiling Fox walked on to the stage to receive the award but Shira was full of rage. She couldn't believe she lost to such an artless book. Shira stormed up onto the stage and took the award from Hocking.

One of the losers, Cynthia Eden said, "Oh my god, she's pulling a Parnanormaye."

"What's that?" Asked the other loser Maggie Shayne.

"Like what Kanye did with Taylor Swift but for Paranormal Romance." Eden replied.

The other women sitting in the audience gasped when Shira took the award from Hocking and held the award up like Moses and the Ten Commandments. She pushed a shocked Angie Fox aside who was very afraid of Shira and ran off the stage crying.

Shira held the award higher as the black and gold heart reflected all the shocked faces in the crowd.

Shira scowled at the crowd and said, "Look at all of you, thinking you know love and the darkside. Writing books that lack art and humanity, just preying on fears and desires of the lonely. You have no sense of what art is and no sense of the truth. I live a paranormal romance. You think writing about spirits and love there would be no consequences, you think this is just all fun and games. It's not! My husband is a real ghost and my real love is here and he is angry and so are his friends. You all make money off their suffering, telling their stories for fun, not realizing people like me face the true horrors of having a paranormal romance. And worst of all you don't even reward my suffering, which I turned in to truth and great art. You not only rejected me, you rejected honoring the sprits. You can answer to them."

The dinning room doors slammed closed and the lights dimmed. Shira laughed as thunder vibrated off the wine and martini glasses. The women were petrified; sprit voices started to howl like a scene out of many of their novels.

The award in Shira's hand started to turn red and blood dripped out of it until the golden black heart broke and angry ghoulish spirits flew out.

Many stories involving paranormal romances were about the spirits needing a human heart to feel alive—this was half true. The spirits needed hearts because eating and living inside them gave them great power.

Shira watched all the spirits flying around the room and screamed, "Take their hearts, they don't deserve them."

Amanda Hocking ducked in fright and screamed, but a black spirit resembling Death went down her throat and ripped out her beating heart. The other spirits did the same as all A to F-List romantic and paranormal writers had their hearts ripped out by the angry spirits.

The spirits piled up all of the taken and beating hearts into one area; the pile of hearts started molding into each other taking the shape of human being.

When every heart was taken and dropped in the pile, each spirit Shira let out went inside one heart and the molding of hearts was complete— it was one single human-looking body of bloody bleeding hearts.

They stood up and stumble walked over toward Shira.

She smiled at the heart body; she was happy to finally be at one with her husband and the spirits. She went to kiss the head of the body of hearts but it sucked the skin off her face and absorbed it, creating facial skin for itself.

In shock and pain Sharia screamed, "Why? I loved you. I loved all of you."

"We need skin."

"But my husband."

"He's in heaven, we're not...we need more skin." The heart body answered back as all of Shia's skin was ripped off her bones, covering the heart body.

Shira died looking at the bald heart body of spirits that deceived her; she had been making love to many spirits but none were her husband.

All the romance writers were dead, some ended up in heaven, but most in hell.

The only person still alive was Fabio who was shaking, hiding under a chair.

The heart body walked toward him, looked down at him, and told Fabio, "We need hair."

New Jersey JuggaloB4Hoes Chatroom Transcript

ThatClownMakeUpOnYourFaceIsMyCum:
Hey fags!!! Stop sucking each other's dicks and listen the fuck up! The greatest musical act in the galaxy is coming to Jersey. That is right cockwads! The Insane fucking Clown Posse! Ever since I saw it posted on their MySpace Page I have been waking up with a raging boner.

SlimShadySucksDicksJuggalo4ForLife:
Fuck yeah! New Jersey JuggalosB4Hoes for life! Fuck mother fucking yeah!!!!!!!!!!!!!!!!!! I saw that shit too: I was so stoked I spent the whole day throwing bottles at school busses. I had to huff paint thinner just to calm the fuck down.

Todd:
Hey guys I'm excited too; my dad is even going to come. We bought clown paint together at Target. It's gonna be super sweet.

ThatClownMakeUpOnYourFaceIsMyCum:
You are such a fag Todd.

SlimShadySucksDicksJuggalo4Life:

Yeah Todd, I bet your dad is gonna have sex with you, cause he is a fag too. You both have fag genes.

Todd:
Guys. I said to stop saying my dad molests me. He is a dentist and likes baseball.

ThatClownMakeUpOnYourFaceIsMyCum:
Yeah he bases your balls in his mouth.

SlimShadySucksDicksJuggalo4Life:
Yeah and pubes too haha!!!!!!

ThatClownMakeUpOnYourFaceIsMyCum:
LOL! Yeah, he makes his own floss out of your pubes.

SlimShadySucksDicksJuggalo4Life:
Yeah Todd you are a dick floss.

Todd:
Hey, stop guys. I am a loyal Juggalo and secretary of The New Jersey JuggalosB4Hoes. We are Juggalo brothers we got to have each other's back. I am still getting beat up at school by JuggaloHataz.

ThatClownMakeUpOnYourFaceIsMyCum:

Chill out Todd and plug up your bleeding vagina.

SlimShadySucksDicksJuggalo4Life:
Yeah Todd, go to the dentist and have your dad give you an
anal filling and stop being such a fag. Juggalos got to be willing
to get beat up by the Hataz.

Todd:
I got stuffed in a locker and they keep calling me clown cum
stain.

ThatClownMakeUpOnYourFaceIsMyCum:
Todd, you should get strapped and shoot them in the head.

SlimShadySucksDicksJuggalo4Life:
Yeah, do a Columbine Todd. Sacrifice your self. If u did you
would be known as Juggalo Jesus.

Todd:
Sometimes I do think about doing it. I have never told
anyone...It is just getting harder, Guys. I can't keep facing it
every day.

ThatClownMakeUpOnYourFaceIsMyCum:
You can't keep your dad's dick in your ass anymore.

SlimShadySucksDicksJuggalo4Life:

Haha! Yeah, you are worthless Todd. You should just off yourself and kill them

Todd:

I think about taking my dad's shotgun for deer hunting and just ending it all..

SlimShadySucksDicksJuggalo4Life:

Yeah, Todd, you should. Go kill yourself and somebody.

Todd:

...All I have is the Juggalos—I've always liked clowns...but the Juggalos...none of you guys like me, no one thinks I'm cool. Even my Juggalo brothers think I am lame and my dad...he looks at me like a disappointment...you guys are right, I really should just fucking end it. It will always be this way.

SlimShadySucksDicksJuggalo4Life:

Wait...what the fuck....Stop this fag talk Todd! This pussy stuff is fucking weird man. It's not cool bro.

ThatIsNotClownMakeUpOnYourFaceItsMyCum:

Yeah Todd, stop being a fag we are just fucking around. You don't want to miss the concert. Come on bro.

Todd:

It won't be fun; I'll be picked on there just like everywhere else...If there is a Heaven I bet it really is like Juggalo Island. I bet it is better than here. I want, to be on that Island, but it doesn't exist. Maybe only in Heaven is where the Juggalos are even nice to each other...My dad has these pills...if you take too many...you don't wake up.

ThatClownMakeUpOnYourFaceIsMyCum:

Dude, stop talking this gay shit and hook us up, bring them to the concert. We can all get fucked up at the show. They sound like awesome downers.

Todd:

... : (

Todd:

I'm sorry guys....I can't bring them cause I just took them all. I am not going to the show. Do you think they let you wear clown make up in Heaven guys? Of course they do. Heaven is a happy Juggalo Island. It has to be.

SlimShadySucksDicksJuggalo4Life:

Stop fucking with us Todd! This is not funny!

Todd:

It feels good. I drank them all with orange soda. I can already feel myself getting sleepy. It can be like the Juggalo dream, but real. If not, then at least I will not wake up and face it.

ThatClownMakeUpOnYourFaceIsMyCum:
This really is not funny Todd!! You are being a total fag. We were kidding. Stop this! Stop fucking around!

Todd:
You know, you were my only real friends, but you guys aren't even nice to me. Even my own Juggalos act like jerks. I have no one. I like the idea of never waking up.

ThatClownMakeUpOnYourFaceIsMyCum:
Dude, stop it, this is really fucked up, we are sorry Todd come on man. The show! The Show!

SlimShadySucksDicksJuggalo4Life:
Make yourself puke. Stop it Todd. Call the fucking police, and get your stomach pumped!

Todd:
No. I puke everyday on my way to school. I am sick of puking. I want to feel good and not want to puke. I am ready to go the Juggalo Island in the Sky. Good Bye guys...

SlimShadySucksDicksJuggalo4Life:
Todd no! Stop!!!!

ThatClownMakeUpOnYourFaceIsMyCum:
Todd, I'm....

Todd: (Has signed off.)

The Rat's Mouth: A Boca Raton Noir

The door to my room at the Whitehall Nursing Home opens; it makes that same death-is-coming-creak it always does as that scumbag Solemnberg walks in.

He gives the same putz look he always does and says, "Hey, Sy. You ready old friend? You, me, and The Jets."

"I guess, so. Grab a seat, Randy." I tell him as he sits by my bedside while the TV is playing.

"Thanks for the invite; it's good to watch the game with someone from the old neighborhood."

"I hear ya, I'm sick of these damn turncoat Dolphin fans...they stink, but hey you me we will always be two Bronx boys, we have no choice but to stick together."

"Stuck here in freakin Boca Raton." He says as we watch The Jets run onto the field, "Here in the 'Rat's Mouth', the Spanish should have called this 'puertas de la muerte'."

"Hey, none of that crap in here, English or Yiddish, these Spanish...too many of them down here."

"Yeah but the women, oy vay."

"What women? You got Samantha Kleinman, the tuckus on her...she was so beautiful, you were the envy of the neighborhood." I tell him shaking my head at him, feeling annoyed of lack of gratitude.

"Eh, after five years of marriage I met a Spanish girl from Harlem, she made Samantha look like a Kugel."

"You schmuck, you went and got tacos on the side."

"Don't judge me. No matter how good the Matzo Ball Soup is you get sick of the same thing."

I shake my head and say, "Here eat some pudding; God rest your wife's soul. She was a good woman."

The game starts as he takes the opened pudding from me and I hand him a spoon.

"Yeah, I know...I hope she can't look down and hear us; she never knew about the girls on the side, the kids either." He looks away from the game and stares down at the pudding and asks, "What did you put in here, extra fiber?"

"Yeah, but it's better than prunes."

"I can't eat that crap, it looks like Oompa Loompa Balls."

"Ha, Solemnberg you're still the damn class clown."

"I have moments; but my girls don't like my jokes."

"You got two pretty daughters, pretty girls don't have to laugh at bad jokes."

"True, how are your girls?"

I feel a sharp pain at the question and just want him to shut up and eat the pudding but tell him, "Ever since Evelyn died they just grieve and eat; the two of them are still with the same schmucks."

"Too bad. Evelyn was nice; a big girl but she had a big heart to go with it."

"My wife ate herself to death. Your wife, dying so soon, now that's tragic; she had the biggest heart."

He laughs and says, "oy, when you're old you can say whatever you want. No one cares, your story is written."

I let out smile and look at the letter I wrote earlier on my nightstand and respond, "Maybe, go eat up before the game starts."

He takes a bite and the years of bitterness I swallow with him watching it go down into his stomach as he says, "Fiber, huh? It really tastes like shit; better make me take a good one."

"You don't know anything about eating shit."

He gives me a funny look and says, "Why you say that? I'm a Jet fan, all I know is how to eat shit."

I snarl at him, "Shut up! No you don't! All my life I ate shit, while I watched you nibble on the best things and sit at the best tables."

He puts the pudding down and says with a drop of sweat falling to his shoe, "What are you talking about?"

I grit my teeth and tell him, "Do you know what it's like to see someone for seventy-something years who you know you are better than end up having the life you wished for?"

More sweat drops from his face and he gives me a nervous smile, "Stop this, it's not funny...what, cause I got Samantha?"

"You got everything, the better wife, the better school, the better kids, the better life and you don't even appreciate it."

"Stop, you're..."

"Saying it like it is; I loved Samantha but instead I got that fat cow of a wife and lousy daughters, lousy jobs. I should have had your life. And I can't have it now, but I can take it away."

"What hell are you saying, Sy? You're lost it."

I take the letter I wrote from the nightstand and put it on my bed.

I pick up the same poisoned pudding, take a bite, and tell him, "In this letter is your suicide and murder note: how you poisoned yourself and me because I was a better man than you and it drove you mad. Mad with guilt. That you screwed me over, lied, cheated, to get where you are today and why I didn't get to that same place."

"You're crazy."

"No, I'm fed up with it all and ready to go. I'm ready to die with the respect and pity I deserve and take away the life of yours that should have been mine."

The poison starts to work as I watch him try to scream but it's too late; I changed his story, made his last moments as bad as my whole life.

Mohammed Is The New Black

The prisoners were sitting in rows and not rioting because of the many guards with guns. The event, *Playwriting for Prisoners* was being held at Bakersfield Penitentiary in Southern California and was soon to start. The news of this play had reached the blogospheres out side of the cell walls causing quite a stir because of the writer/director/actor of the play.

This man known as Sam Bacille born Nakoula Basseley Nakoula, had converted his controversial YouTube video *Innocence of The Muslims* into a play for his fellow prisoners and the warden gave it the green light. Under California Law 4A6, Prisoner's were allowed artistic expression and were protected under the First Amendment.

Sam took advantage of this law and got The Aryan Brotherhood to help star and produce in his first feature play. This act and enthusiasm by the white supremacists showed a great sociological change and maybe even tolerance in the Southern California prison system.

Though born in Egypt and not technically 'white' Sam was a hero to the Aryan Brotherhood for "pissing off sand niggers everywhere" and became the one and only non-white members of the Aryan Brotherhood.

For the Brotherhood, hating kikes and niggers was staring to feel redundant; their priorities of who to hate had taken a different turn after 9/11. Not only were they worried about 'Sand Niggers' flying planes into white men's proud and tall white built buildings, but the Neo-Nation of Islam was making a comeback into the penal system.

Islam was now the white man's biggest threat all over the world, the Jews second, and non-Muslim blacks third.

These circumstances lead Sam to become the only member of the Aryan Brotherhood born in Africa who was not South African. The white men found him admirable and even useful—the same way Hitler looked at the Japanese.

Sam also brought with him many useful skills. The Aryan Christian men struggled to read but Sam could read and teach them the Bible and was really good at telling stories why the Muslims were so evil and why Christian men needed to stick together.

His speeches were *Hitleresque* when speaking of the Muslims and it gave The Aryan brotherhood a morale boost.

Hitler never matched the Aryan ideal either, but like Sam he was such a good speaker that none of the NAZI's noticed. Colored or not, Sam needed the Brotherhood and they needed him. They also liked knowing somebody who got over 10 million views on YouTube.

But letting a *colored* in was a slippery white slope. The Aryans were outnumbered and were the minority in jail and noticed the Mexicans also shared Sam's passion for Jesus; they had many tattoos of a white Jesus on their arms and chest. They always were in good shape, had good drug connections, and didn't like Islam either as when they had squabbles with the Nation of Islam they would say, 'Mohammed es el Diablo'.

The Aryans thought Mohammed was of Satan too; maybe the Mexicans weren't as bad as they thought. Sam wasn't so bad for one who lacked pure blood. They liked Jesus, Sam liked Jesus and the Mexicans were the least dark of all the colored.

More importantly an alliance with them would be equal to the number of black Muslims.

Though not possessing a high combined average IQ, the Aryan Brotherhood accepted they needed the Mexicans. They were the true new Japanese, the white man needed to survive and at least they worshiped Jesus and also hated that sand nigger terrorist Mohammed.

The big question was how to set up an alliance with them. Once again the Brotherhood saw Sam's usefulness.

Though not men who loved the high arts, the Aryan Brotherhood knew that movies and art had power and admired that Sam pissed off so many Muslims because of his movie trailer. The Aryan Brotherhood were also big Russell Crowe fans and for most of them, their favorite cinematic scene was the curb scene in American History X—they did not like the second and third act of the film but loved the first and many watched the white friendly edited version online.

Movies and art were the best recruitment tools and form of manipulation for the Aryan Brotherhood and with Sam ready to perform his play they were ready to appeal to the Mexicans and piss off the black Muslims.

The black Muslims were not pleased to be sitting there to watch these white devils do this marked man's play—there was a steep jihad placed on Sam Bacille. The Mexicans on the other hand were in the back and very curious to see Sam's play.

Even surrounded by white guards with guns, the black Muslims couldn't help but act restless; they sat there knowing they were soon about to watch blasphemy.

The most well read leader Mohammed Shabaz Jenkins shared the group's discontent, "I don't want to see that Rushdie movie writing mother fucker. We got a jihad on his ass."

There were claps from the black Muslims upfront, but that Rushdie motherfucker paid them no mind and was ready to share the truth of the Holy Spirit through his art. Sam Bacille and his fellow Aryan brother stood with pride at the side of the stage wearing outfits for the play.

The warden then came out onto the stage and quitted the crowd.

Warden Karl Talls liked Sam in secret. He was happy and even proud he had a true hero in his prison. Warden Talls was of one the first *Birthers*; the only people he hated more than President Obama were other Muslims. He knew he owed Jesus and the prisoners to see the truth of the demonic religion known as Islam.

On top of the stage he told the restless prisoners, "Alright, now we got us here a world renown writer, boys. So y'all need to show some respect and be polite for Sam Bacille's play, *The Innocence*. Do your play son, and God bless ya."

Sam nodded with approval while there were grunts from the black Muslims. Sam did not care about the groans; he smiled at the crowd and said with his Egyptian-American accent, "Good evening, as many of you know, I produced a passion film that never saw the light of day, but thanks to my friends here and good hearted warden, we shall finish its final scene. Here is the *Innocence of the Muslims*."

Sam stayed on stage as a white man with long blond hair joined him. It was hard to tell if it was wig or if he was the Aryan brother who was allowed to grow his hair out—to make sure the white men stayed pure even if engaging in homosexuality.

Sam laid out an African blanket with the longhaired white man; they rested on the blanket and began the play.

The longhaired white man said in a feminine voice to Sam, "Oh Hello Mohammed, how is it going deceiving the stupid Arabs that you're a prophet for God?"

"Excellent, my old crusty satanic lover."

"Good, I am glad you told them that Satan told you to say you worship those other gods instead of Allah. It makes it look more believable. Now they'll never expect that Satan is really behind your teachings"

"Yes, my menopausal wife. The Arabs are much more stupid than the Jews..."

A man from the Nation of Islam screamed, "This is terrible. This is worse than The Jews."

But the Mexicans clapped and laughed as one said, "Mohammed el Diablo. Gusto! Gusto!"

Sam winked at the Mexicans in the audience and said, "Si, and yes, my love Khadija; Satan has been so helpful in helping us deceive the Arabs, soon our Satanic religion will spread everywhere and even surpass Christianity and even the American negroes who are lesser brained will be duped by our religion."

"Ah hell no! This just wrong," One of The Nation Of Islam screamed.

"You quiet down now boy." The warden said.

A guard held up his shotgun and Mohammed Shabaz Jenkins silenced himself, holding his arms while looking at the stage with disgust.

Sam continued, "Yes, Khadija, Hell awaits us; The Dark Lord will treat us well."

"Oh Mohammed, you're so smart to have all of the Muslims follow us to Hell. Satan will be so pleased."

"Yes, they will follow us but we won't be able to stop Jesus from reaching the smart Spanish people in Mexico. They are very good people who believe in Jesus Christ. They will be saved from Hell."

The Mexicans whistled and others said Rosary prayers, while the members of Nation of Islam were gritting their teeth in hatred. Many of the Muslims were asking Allah to keep them from murdering Sam and one of the young lifer Muslims was taking out a shank and asking Allah if He wanted him to throw it at that moment.

The white long haired man playing Khadija continued "I am so much older than you, who will be your new wife when I die and I am in Hell waiting for you?"

"You're very old, that is why I will marry a 10 year old who can give me children. Allah Hu Akbar."

It was the final straw and the young Muslim with the shank also said "Allah Hu Akbar!" and threw his shank at the stage.

It missed Sam but caught the longhaired white man playing Khadija right in the neck. Blood spilled out as the actor was really entering the afterlife and most likely going to Hell.

But Sam did not stop his play. Even as fights broke out in the crowd between white and black, he ad-libbed, "Yes, a holy war will come and blood will be spilled. The Muslims will pay. God will punish them from high. Praise Jesus! Let the Holy war begin." Sam then looked at The Mexicans in the back and said, "Join us *muchacos! Luchar por Christo*!"

The Varg Vikernes Parole Hearing

Author's Note

Varg Vikernes was a member of the Norway Death Metal Band *Mayhem*. He went to prison because he burned churches, killed his bandmate, and made soup of his brain.

He recently had a parole hearing. Here is a transcript of the hearing that was not made public.

****

Case 453 Oslo Norway,
Audio Transcription from Transcriber and Metal Fan (Silje Axness)

Silje Axness: Defendant valks into the room vearing a Viking Hat and a Shirt that says 'Christianity Is a Jewish Abortion.' Defendant vis very brutal and beautiful. Vere are three-parole board members vere to judge Varg Vikernes. Blessed is his birth name by Satan and Odin who goes by alias Count Grishnakh! Vey are vools of the state if vey do not appreciate the glory of such a brutal black metal genius.

Parole Officer 1: Good Vorning Vister Vikernes. Today is your parole hearing; how are vou today?

Varg Vikernes: I am death metal super star and prophet of Odin. I am of the pure Nordic race. I vas in most brutal band in world. Now, I am just alive, vich is never good, but blessed by Satan and Odin I will be free to serve them.

Parole Officer 2: Vuy are up for parole now; ve must ask you about your past crimes. The other officers want to know the origin of the murder of your bandmate Euronymous. Having served your penance and do you feel contrition?

Varg Vikernes: Zee Murder was done with love and unselfishness. Contrition is not needed.

Parole Officer 1: Love? Your band and your action is anything but...please explain.

Varg Vikernes: Vell you vool, our old member Dead, vas so brutal and found the world so boring and stupid he decided he vanted to be with Satan and Lord Odin and killed himself. So out of love, I killed Euronymous so Dead would have good friend in Hell. Bless them both in the name of Satan and Odin.

Parole Officer 2: Ves, I know the story you and your band mates took pictures for album cover and rumored to make soup of his brains.

Varg Vikernes: Ves, it is true. The mind carries energy. Ve Vanted to keep Euronymous *brutalness* while his soul burned in hell. So ve had brain soup in honor of Odin and Lord Satan.

Parole Officer 1: Vhat does this disturbing act have to do vith the murder of Euronymous? How do you state this act was of good will? It is appalling?

Varg Vikernes: No. Dead was true brutal death metal artist, vut even the strongest get lonely in Hell. Euronymous vas becoming less brutal. He did not vant to burn down churches anymore but drink and play scrabble vith his girlfriend instead. I vas trying to help them both. I did not vant Dead to be in Hell alone so I made Euronymous dead to be with Dead and to stop him from becoming a weakling of the living. Now Euronymous is in Hell being trained by Death, Satan, and Lord Odin to be brutal again.

Parole Officer 2: You mentioned Church burnings and you are still a practicing Satanist. Vould you burn down churches again?

Varg Vikernes: No, that is not brutal anymore; Satan and Odin vould find that very 10 years ago. I vould show my love to my Dark Masters by running for Government to help carry out brutal policies.

Parole Office 1: Do you have anti-Semitic beliefs?

Varg Vikernes: Ves. The Jews gave birth to the weakest religion Christanity and we now do not worship the great Odin or Satan. My platform vould be anti-Jew, Christian, and Muslim and I vould like to kill the sick and most babies for vey are worthless and not very brutal.

Parole Officer 2: Do you belong in society sir?

Varg Vikernes: Ves, to destroy and bring forth Odin's reign with the fallen angel Lucifer. I will make sure life vis brutal for all in back in society.

Parole Officer 1:Vou keep saying the word *Brutal*; vhat is this brutal? I do not understand.

Varg Vikernes: Brutal, is vhat is in my blood. If life not brutal, vis mistake.

Parole Officer 2: So you vant a life of public service? Do vou know politicians and government workers like ourselves vust not be in trouble and public eye?

Varg Vikernes: Yah, I von't start apocalypse until I president of Norway and make The God worshipers and humanists sacrifice vemselves for Odin.

Parole Officer 1: Good to hear sir Varg.

Parole Officer 2: Yah, vou are ready, vou have passed all test. Ve NAZI Satanist Viking party of Norway veels vou're the one run for office.

Parole Officer 2: Yah, Norway has become weak and we need to become Nordic Vikings again and control the world like ve once did, ve must be blessed by great God Odin and vallen angel Lucifer. Type Girl stand up, vou know vhy vou here.

Silje Axness: Yah. I shall be vour vessel to help vring Anti-Christ through seed of Varg Vikernes.

Parole Officer: Come have sex vith new *Fuher*; you shall carry the seed of ve savior of Norway.

Varg Vikernes: Yah Brutal.

The Little Drone That Could: A Children's Story

Drew The Drone didn't fit in with all the other drones.

But he was special, he looked like a magical pigeon from a magical land called Lahore, Pakistan.

Being a drone was a super special job given by Papa Obama where all the drones would get to play and fly in the sky finding bad men with beards send them to a sleepaway camp in the sky—where the bad men would no longer be bad.

It was a sky higher than any drone could fly.

Drew The Drone lived on the border of a magical place in Pakistan, where he was near his American best friends in Afghanistan.

But this border had a lot of meanies living on it. These bearded meanies would shoot at anything looking like a drone or any Lahore Pigeon because the bearded meanies liked shoot birds or anything that was flying above them because that is what meanies do.

Drew knew about these meanies because his older Drone brothers and pigeons were shot down and hurt by the meanie bearded men and could never fly again. The bearded men did not want to go to sleepaway camp so they were even bigger meanies to all the drones.

This made Drew mad because that he couldn't play with all the other Drones.

Drew's daddy, Papa Obama had made a daddy decision to protect his favorite and only pigeon drone Drew.

Papa Obama said Drew should stay at home all day in their magical cave while the other Drones got to play and send the bearded men and sometimes non-bearded men to sleepaway camp in the sky.

Papa Obama told the other drones not to get sad if they took the wrong people to sleepaway camp, that it was okay and he still loved them the same.

He also reminded Drew that is was okay that he didn't get to play with the other drones. That Papa Obama still loved him and one day because of Drew being special and different he would help not just Papa Obama but all of his human brothers and sisters in America.

Drew wanted to believe in Papa Obama's words but he would forget them when the other Drones shaped like planes would laugh and be meanies to Drew. They called him meanie names like Cavebird.

It made Drew the Drone very sad.

Drew wanted to fly with other Drones and send the bearded bad men to sleepaway camp but Papa Obama wouldn't let him out of fear losing his favorite drone.

Papa Obama knew Drew was special, but Drew started to believing he wasn't.

Drew the Drone became more sad when he heard the other Drones come back to the magic cave and say how they sent 12 bearded men and a few non-bearded humans to the special sleepaway camp in the sky with their magic lasers.

Drew started to feel even more in dumps, when he gathered with his brothers to get a special message from Papa Obama.

A magical movie screen was kept in the cave where they learned about all the meanie bearded men. Papa Obama appeared on the magical screen and told his Drones how proud he was of them and they were doing a great job stopping the meanie-bearded men. He reminded his drones how bad the meanies were because they wanted to hurt their favorite character in the whole wide world—Aladdin.

They loved Aladdin and Papa Obama reminded them that if Aladdin was to live, all the bearded men had to go away to sleepaway camp, but since they were doing such a good job Aladdin would live forever.

They all smiled and cheered but Papa Obama saw his favorite Pigeon drone Drew was sad.

He told the other Drones to have a pleasant sleep and wished those who had night patrol good luck. They all left but Papa Obama told Drew to stay.

He gave Drew a fatherly smile, "Drew, you look down. Tell Papa Obama what is the matter?"

Drew sulked and said, "Papa, I just...I want to play outside with the other Drones. Every night before I power down I hear about all the bearded men they sent to sleepaway camp...and golly gee, I haven't even sent one, and shucks, I just want to do you proud Papa Obama. And Christmas coming real soon, and I wanted to send a bearded meanie man to sleepaway camp as Christmas gift to you papa."

Papa Obama gave Drew a thoughtful head nod on the cave screen and said, "Look, Drew, I understand. And that is a thoughtful Christmas gift. I know things have been very hard, little buddy, but I keep you safe in the cave because I love you. Look, son, I know the other Drones get to have more fun and send more bearded meanies to sleepaway camp but I promise you, I will call on you on a special day and you will do something very special Drew. I promise you that, son."

"Ok Papa Obama. I trust you papa. I look forward to and wait for that day."

"That is the spirit Drew, trust me, one day you'll see why you're my favorite Drone. For now we just need to worry about making sure America has the best Christmas ever."

Drew's magical mechanics made him give a half-hearted smile as Papa Obama said goodnight and the screen went blank. Drew went to bed and powered down to dream of puppy dogs and ice cream cones.

When he awoke and powered up, he saw most of brothers staring at him with meanie faces.

His least favorite brother John McDrone was practicing his flying and said to Drew, "We overheard you last night. So you're papa's favorite? I don't think so. You haven't even sent one of the bearded men to sleepaway camp with your magical lasers in your mouth."

The rest of the drones flapped their wings feeling bad they were not Papa Obama's favorite. Drew did not like this meanie look of all his brothers but didn't want to be a meanie too and said, "Guys, Papa was trying to make me feel better, it's not true."

Drew's big drone heart lied to make his brothers and sisters feel better because unlike them he was not a meanie.

John McDrone stopped flying and said, "That's how good Papa Obama is, he even makes doodyhead drones like Drew feel better."

"YEAH WE LOVE PAPA OBAMA." All The Drones said and were about to laugh and play when Papa Obama appeared on screen.

He looked upset and said to his beloved Drone children, "Hello, my children. I have very sad news. You're American brothers have all been destroyed."

The Drones were shocked. It couldn't be true.

John McDrone wanted to cry with the other sad drones but he asked Papa Obama, "Why Papa? Why would someone want to hurt us? We take the bearded men to sleepaway camp where they play with puppies and drink lemonade when it gets too hot."

"And it's going be Christmas tomorrow, Papa Obama, why would someone do this before Christmas?" Drew the Drone said with a sob.

"I know boys. I'm very upset too. It is a Grinch named Rand Paul. He got both parties to pass a Drone rule in your land of birth, America. It's terrible what they did to all your brothers. They have now gone to their own sleepaway camp in a far far away land.."

"NO!" They said in unison.

"Yes boys and even worse, I need a drone here because a bearded man is here and he is very suspicious and could hurt my other children—the American People."

"NO PAPA OBAMA!"

"Who is this meanie?" John McDrone asked.

"He is from Pakistan, in Lahore. He is here supposedly doing a reading but my hardworking Gnomes at the NSA say he is meanie adult word *A Reluctant Fundamentalist* and from what the elves have seen in his e-mails he is dangerous bearded man. He is bearded meanie sounding name too— Moshin Hamid."

"OH NO!"

"Yes, the gnomes of the NSA told me so; they are never wrong. He is here in America and the gnomes say he is meeting with a meanie bearded man on Christmas day in New

York City. Who would not celebrate Christmas but the most evil of men? This Moshin Hamid could do very bad things, and we need to send to sleepaway camp before he sends all of American."

"OH NO!"

"Oh yes, boys. Unfortunately, I can't have any real looking Drones come over, as they will stand out and be shot down."

"OH NO!"

"Yes, but Drew looks like a Pigeon and New York is full of them. So Drew you must come fly over to New York City and stop this Moshin Hamid cause I fear his reluctant fundamentalism, which is the adult word for meanie and suspicious activity."

"OH NO!" Drew said with the other drones. But after the super sad news Drew realized he was going to get his chance to show he was a special and make Papa Obama proud.

The Drones were shocked and even more scared when they understood the truth that only Drew could save America and even more important—Christmas.

But Papa Obama had faith in Drew and knew he was special because he knows everything thanks to the magical gnomes and elves at the NSA.

Papa Obama's face stayed serious and said, "I know you guys give ribbing to Drew for being different, but I want you learn a valuable lesson, that being different is good and can make you special. This meanie Moshin Hamid I believe to be part of a sleeper sell of the bearded men, and I think he is gathering with another secret bearded men to do something very bad on Christmas. The gnomes of the NSA are never wrong. They say he is going to read from a meanie book that makes many meanie men and he's going to do it on Christmas with other meanies."

"OH NO!"

"Drew you must fly over right now and stop Moshin Hamid, you must send him to sleepaway camp with the other bearded men using your magical lasers."

John McDrone looked at Drew and said, "Save Christmas, Drew. Save America."

Drew smiled and flapped his wings, "I will. I will make you guys proud. I can do it with your help, Papa Obama."

"Yes we can." Papa Obama said and smiled.

Drew took the magical words from Papa Obama and flapped his wings into the night sky. He knew he to fly high, were the angels and plans are to not be shot down by the bearded men.

Drew was going to show that Papa Obama was right; he knew it was his chance to save Christmas.

He flew deep into the fog as Christmas Eve was ending and Christmas day was beginning. Papa Obama watched Drew fly through his magic cameras; Drew looked like a real pigeon so the evil Grinch Rand Paul would not shoot him down.

Even when he became tired Drew the Drone still flew fast over the seas, until he saw the magical Empire State building of New York and all the pigeons chirped to welcome to best place in the world, America. He felt the land's magic in his solar powered soul and was ready to save the beloved city of New York.

Papa Obama and his commanders sent magical messages to make sure Drew the Drone flew to Union Square where they saw Moshin Hamid was there with another bearded meanie man.

Drew and Papa Obama were ready to stop them and save Christmas.

Through his magical camera powers Papa Obama could see through Drew's eyes. He saw the meanie Moshin Hamid; who was not drinking eggnog but tea—which is not very Christmas-like.

Using the same magic, Drew's eyes helped them use facial recognition and saw that it was a meanie named Salmon Rushdie who Papa Obama realized was a traitor and spy for all the bearded man. He knew this to be true because the NSA gnomes told him so. For Papa Obama knew all.

And Papa Obama knew he had to stop them and save Christmas and only Drew the Drone could do that.

Drew landed on top of a tree looking down at the meanie Mohsin Hamid. He was standing while the other sat reading a book and drinking tea of this warm Christmas day.

Drew knew the bearded men were bad people by just seeing them not celebrating Christmas. These were the real bad meanie bearded men.

Drew the Drone stayed quiet but the meanie Mohsin Hamid looked up and said to the other bearded man, "It is a miracle. How beautiful, a Lahore Pigeon! Come here, you beautiful bird, I shall feed you bread."

Drew felt his wings flap without thinking of it. He landed on the Mohsin's shoulder and made a nice chirp. Hamid's friend Salman Rushdie smiled and Drew felt a love he was surprised to feel for the two bearded meanie men.

The meanie Moshin Hamid was not much of meanie at all but as he and his friend Salman petted Drew's magical feathers Papa Obama spoke in his ear, "Look, Drew I just want to tell you I am proud of you and I want to say goodbye. You will be taking Mohsin Hamid and his friend Salmon Rushdie to sleepaway camp. The gnomes and elves from the NSA have looked at what these men wrote, they are very dangerous and you must take them now. Goodbye Drew. You were my favorite Drone."

Before Drew could say goodbye a magical sparkle shot out of him and he took the Moshin Hamid and Salman Rushdie to that special sleepaway camp in the sky.

Secret Bonus Story

Phonedicks

At first it seemed like a cruel prank, maybe even something out of *The Onion*, but then eyes started missing, ears were punctured, and deaths pilled up.

Cellphones dropped to the ground and semen leaked out of them.

Even if you used a Bluetooth, it could happen to you: a dick could jump out of your cellphone and kill you.

Why dicks were attacking the innocent no one knew; the origin of the killer cellphone dicks was still trying to be figured out by phone providers working with scientists.

It seemed preposterous, but the police saw enough bodies and knew this was either a cult, a deadly malfunction, or dicks really were jumping out of cellphones and attacking people.

The evidence showed semen on every cellphone where a murder took place; it appeared that when the dicks popped out of the phone so did semen, but these dicks weren't sexual; they were not out to do sexual things.

No, they were an angry and violent species, like they had been imprisoned and tortured for many years and needed to kill once they popped out of a cellphone.

Sometimes they would shoot semen again at their victims but it was only used as a weapon, a way to blind their prey if they weren't already poked in the eye by the killer dick.

Word spread.

Detectives started accepting the theory of killer cellphone-dicks.

They used email and barely texted feeling suspicious and afraid to be near a cellphone.

Non-officers couldn't believe that dicks could come out of a phone, but more and more attacks were happening.

Officers and Government Officials pondered even more worrisome thoughts: where did the dicks go after they killed? Did they go back into the cellphone or did they hide? Were the dicks planning something together? Could there be a massive attack of dicks?

The questions lingered as more learned and believed the hypothesis of the killer cellphone-dicks. The information traveled up the food chain of power, as many men and women of influence were suspicious and worried about this phenomenon but were too afraid to use their phones to talk about it.

These men and women of power started using Morse code to communicate, and even a few debated on doing a Public Service Announcement but all the major phone companies used their lobbyists to influence Congress, and no PSA was made and more cellphone dick deaths increased.

It took only a few days before for the first dick phone attack was caught on camera.

An American man was porn-Skyping to a Russian-immigrant on a sex cam; she asked him to take his dick out, but he said he felt shy and told her he had a pic in his phone and he could send it to her.

He picked up his iPhone and opened it when an erect penis jumped out of the phone screen with semen leaking out; the dick went straight into the man's nostrils.

The sex cam worker screamed and watched in horror as a skinny dick dug deep into the man's nostrils stabbing him in the brain.

The bloody dick then slithered out of the man's right ear and was not viewed again.

No one could tell if it went back into the phone or if it slithered out of the man's apartment.

One of the head detectives on the crime scene just shrugged his shoulders and said: *it was mystery...or a dickery.*

The video was leaked onto the Internet but many watched it on their cellphones. Some would see the dick attack the man and then it happened to them.

There were many more deaths as the dicks jumped out of the phone like a hologram coming to life when the head hit the air, always leaving semen behind as it went straight to the face for the kill.

Some tried to bite the dick in defense, but these dicks didn't want oral pleasure; they only wanted to bring death. They didn't care how they killed; they went deep into the throat to make victims choke to death. They were rubbery and made teeth a useless weapon against these pissed off dicks.

Where the dicks ended up after the attacks, no one knew; some theorized they were not dicks but maybe a technological worm that came to life, or maybe a new kind of snake, but the labs showed that all the victims were attacked by dicks, as foreskin was left on the victims and semen was always on the cell phone.

They realized these dicks were not circumcised and highly dangerous.

The only motive and lead they had were that the dicks came from cell phones, and there was a much higher percentage of male victims than women.

The cellphones of the victims were confiscated and locked up; scientists from the military wore protective gear and tried to open up the phones of potential cellphone dicks, but once the dick popped out it was unstoppable and could find a way to kill—no object could protect you from a killer dick attack.

All that was left was semen and blood, as the killer dicks never appeared again.

The Government looked everywhere using Homeland Security, checking sewers, and even scuba divers checked the ocean but they couldn't find one single cellphone dick.

The only thing those privileged enough to know the truth about the cellphone dicks was to make sure their kids didn't have any cellphones in their house and pray not to encounter anyone who does.

But that wasn't enough, and as the knowledge spread, something had to be done to stop these killer dicks.

The Department of Defense and Human Health Services tried to team up and stop the dickphone epidemic; they pleaded with President Obama but he felt it was too rash and he needed more proof stating this sounded like the idea of a crazy conspiracy radio broadcaster.

It was just too illogical for President Obama to accept but Vice President Biden said it made sense to him and thought it could be a plot of The Chinese. He couldn't give a direct order, but he told his staff they needed to follow this threat before America became a blood bath of dicks.

While the vice president respected the danger of the 'dickedemic', many everyday people did not heed the fears of the killer dickphones; they loved their cellphones and the idea sounded like a prank.

They paid for this love with their lives, as many who didn't throw away their cellphones became casualties.

The constant daily deaths affected the youth; nihilism took the culture of the young as they started to get off on purposely seeing if they could face a killer cellphone dick.

Bored college kids started play dickphone roulette: a group would sit and turn the cell phone on, pass it around, and see what would happen.

Some kids faced nothing but a group of college kids at the University of Maryland played it in their dorm room with disastrous results; a freshman named Tiffany Turner, turned on her friend John's cell phone and looked at different photos he had taken.

She saw many pics of him giving the finger until a pic came up of the young man's penis and then the pic became real; it jumped out of the phone, and stabbed her in the eye as blood dripped down her face as semen dripped down from the phone.

The others watched, while John ran out the room knowing the rumors were true. He escaped out of the dorm and made it to the campus police.

The two male police officers listened to the boy cry and nodded their head, both realizing it was true—the cellphone dicks were real.

The police went back, armed and ready, to the boy's dorm room to find his friends were corpses; some had choked to death, others were stabbed—it was clearly the work of a killer cellphone dick.

The head cop reported it and said they had a survivor and even an owner of an alleged dickphone.

The federal government higher ups from the FBI to the CIA took John in and questioned him along with members of the upper echelon of the military and health services to see if they could find a casual relation between the dickphone and the attack.

The boy told them that he kept a cock pic in the phone and when his friend Tiffany saw it, the dick came out of the phone and attacked her.

The military men and health services finally had a hypothesis that made sense: it was the cock pics themselves.

They were coming alive.

Not only was it tasteless to have cock pics, it was also dangerous.

The NSA notified each other. There was a practice of keeping track of cock pics, not for reasons of terrorism just because it seemed like a good idea and private studies showed it kept up NSA worker morale.

The FBI and CIA were given addresses, and in a week all cellphones of known cock pics were taken back to Washington to be examined by the top scientists.

The theory was tested in secret laboratories; scientists wore protective outfits, but the dicks were powerful enough to penetrate those and killed many of the top minds of DC and escaped.

Through trial and error and many more deaths, they learned the dicks could not be shot or sliced to death—they possessed an unreal skin that could burrow itself through a solid object; the only way to kill them was by fire.

Like sausages they could be cooked and killed.

The scientists carried flamethrowers with them but often the dicks were too fast. Many more scientists lost their lives by the killer dicks; if the flames missed the dicks, it only made them angrier and the deaths became more violent.

When the dicks were done killing they slithered out of the protective metal the scientist wore and disappeared from the laboratory.

The new protocol became not to open the cellphones, but to have them all in one place and burn them—a dickphoneocaust.

There was a top-secret laboratory, hidden in the sticks and cornfields of the countryside of Maryland that was 45 minutes outside of DC; the Government planned to cremate up to 10 million phones.

The Government made a deal with the phone companies, they would subsidize their losses until the dickphone ordeal was dealt with and there was a final solution.

The President and Vice President Biden felt this was the best way to avert a national crisis of a nation dying by phonedicks. The Government and phone companies agreed, as confiscating and regulating smart phones was a reasonable compromise.

They sent them all to the top-secret laboratory in Maryland which had a crematory made for any kind of contagion to be eliminated; the design and size of conveyor belt and furnace was inspired by NAZI Germany but the American government felt it would only be used on the diseased and only in dire circumstances.

The Joint Chiefs of Staff and the Vice President were there to follow through on the burning of the phonedicks; President Obama was in a secure location, he still couldn't accept in his logical mind such a preposterous event, but Vice

President Biden could and was there to make sure all the dicks died.

Biden still believed the Chinese were behind it as they refused to work with America and report any known *dicktalities*; he felt he had to handle this, if he was to have any kind of legacy it was to make sure these killer dicks wouldn't pop out of a phone ever again.

He lead the charge against the cell phone dicks; it took a lot of manpower and overtime by the NSA, but all the dick pic phones were confiscated and brought to the secret laboratory and compound in Maryland.

Even Biden had to get rid of his own cellphone.

He and the Joint Chief of Staffs had them all lowered onto the conveyor belt.

The button was pressed and the conveyer belt moved, but when men working security looked at the cameras, they saw movement in the surrounding cornfields; it looked like snakes traveling in packs, but they were not snakes—it was all of the phonedicks coming to save their brethren.

How the dicks knew what was happening and kept themselves hidden all this time was a mystery that no one had time to answer, all the men and women of authority knew was that the cellphone dicks were speeding quickly to the compound.

They were outnumbered and the Vice President knew he had to stop them; he had a fail-proof plan no one knew about, not even President Obama, but he didn't want to enact it unless all else failed.

While the dicks outside came closer, the conveyer belt moved the phones closer to the furnace but the heat and sound made the dicks start to pop out of the phone.

The few soldiers and secret service weren't sure which dicks to fight—the ones coming in, or the ones popping out. They waited for the Vice President to say something but he hid himself in the bathroom as the dicks outside busted through the door.

The soldiers and secret service fired their rounds but the bullets didn't stop the dicks. They saw by their ruthless murders they were something else, something evil.

They weren't human dicks or clones from phones; they were a new form of species. They were asexual dicks out to destroy the human race; they started with the soldiers, then The Chiefs of Staff, and if not stopped, they would destroy all of humanity.

The smarter men of the room realized the cell phone dicks were a form of Singularity: photos and technology mixing together, finding a way to become real to bend physics and reproduce itself out of a phone—a womb for the dick pics, to be three-dimensional beings.

When birthed they only wanted to kill anything that was not of the same species.

Knowing this was futile, as the dicks kept coming, over a million dicks swarmed through the building ready for world domination. They killed all the men and women leaving only a Vice President Biden cowering in the bathroom.

Biden heard the dicks coming; he knew they'd bust through the wall.

He said a prayer asking God to forgive him for his sins, because only an angry God would allow a world full of killer dicks; he asked Him to keep his wife safe and then said, "Alright you dicks, why don't you suck on this."

He kicked the door open and as the dicks shot forward at Biden he opened his shirt showing the dynamite around his chest; he had the military complex design to annihilate anything in a half-mile distance.

The dicks shot forward but they shriveled into ash as Biden pressed the button.

Acknowledgements

There really is only one person to thank and that is Satan. I am your servant Dark Lord. This book is dedicated to you Lucifer.

Final Note

If you love, liked, or hated this book please leave a review; also I really enjoy hate mail and cat/dog pics. You can send whatever you would like to Christophpaulwriter@gmail.com

Just don't Spam me bro,

Christoph Paul

Made in the USA
San Bernardino, CA
27 April 2014